Warpath 2
Deadly Skies

Suddenly I felt a massive *thump*, then an explosion knocked the controls out of my hands. The Spitfire dropped and the cockpit began to fill with smoke. Flames licked around my feet. As I plunged towards the ground I could feel myself starting to lose consciousness. The smoke had now filled the cockpit; I couldn't see anything or scarcely breathe. I didn't know if I was over land or sea; I didn't know my altitude; all I knew for certain was that I'd been hit and I was trapped inside a burning plane.

Read and collect the other books in the
Warpath *series*

1: TANK ATTACK
3: BEHIND ENEMY LINES
4: DEPTH-CHARGE DANGER

WARPATH 2
Deadly Skies

J. ELDRIDGE

A fictional story
based on real-life events

PUFFIN BOOKS

With thanks to Wing Commander Ron Finch

PUFFIN BOOKS

Published by the Penguin Group
Penguin Books Ltd, 27 Wrights Lane, London W8 5TZ, England
Penguin Putnam Inc., 375 Hudson Street, New York, New York 10014, USA
Penguin Books Australia Ltd, Ringwood, Victoria, Australia
Penguin Books Canada Ltd, 10 Alcorn Avenue, Toronto, Ontario, Canada M4V 3B2
Penguin Books (NZ) Ltd, Private Bag 102902, NSMC, Auckland, New Zealand

Penguin Books Ltd, Registered Offices: Harmondsworth, Middlesex, England

First published 1999
5

Copyright © J. Eldridge, 1999
Photographs copyright © the Imperial War Museum
All rights reserved

The moral right of the author has been asserted

Set in 11.5/15pt Monotype Bookman Old Style
Typeset by Rowland Phototypesetting Ltd,
Bury St Edmunds, Suffolk
Printed in England by Clays Ltd, St Ives plc

Except in the United States of America, this book is sold subject
to the condition that it shall not, by way of trade or otherwise, be lent,
re-sold, hired out, or otherwise circulated without the publisher's
prior consent in any form of binding or cover other than that in
which it is published and without a similar condition including this
condition being imposed on the subsequent purchaser

British Library Cataloguing in Publication Data
A CIP catalogue record for this book is available from the British Library

ISBN 0-140-38983-0

Contents

Invasion Britain

The attacks by the German forces at the start of the Second World War had been swift and decisive. By May 1940 they had swept through most of northern Europe: Denmark, Norway, Belgium, Luxemburg, Holland and France. The British Expeditionary Force (BEF), sent to try to stop Hitler's advancing armies, was defeated. About 340,000 mostly British soldiers were evacuated by a flotilla of boats from the French seaport of Dunkirk between the end of May and the start of June.

Less than a year since Britain had declared war on Germany in September 1939, it looked as if Hitler's ambition to conquer Europe was almost complete. Only one country remained unconquered:

Britain – separated from mainland Europe by a narrow strip of water, the English Channel.

Britain was still poorly prepared for war, lacking both the necessary weapons and the resources to defend itself against a strong invader. By July 1940, the German plans for the invasion of Britain – code-named 'Sea-Lion' – were ready.

A series of attacks was to be mounted by the German air force, the Luftwaffe, to destroy Britain's Royal Air Force (RAF). Without the RAF there would be no air cover to defend Britain against a sea invasion. The air attacks were to take place in August. The German army, superior both in numbers and armaments, would then invade across the Channel.

With Britain defeated, the war in Europe would effectively be over. However, the whole operation depended on the destruction of the RAF. Hitler knew this only too well. The opening paragraph of his Directive to his Commanders of 1 August 1940 said: 'Using all possible means, the German air forces will smash the British air forces in as brief a period of time as possible.'

With 3,000 Luftwaffe planes against 620 RAF Spitfires and Hurricanes – and only 1,000 pilots trained to fly them – the scene was set for a fateful encounter in the deadly skies over southern England. Neither side could afford to lose the battle for Britain.

Our story begins in August 1940. A young Spitfire pilot prepares to play his part in the conflict to come.

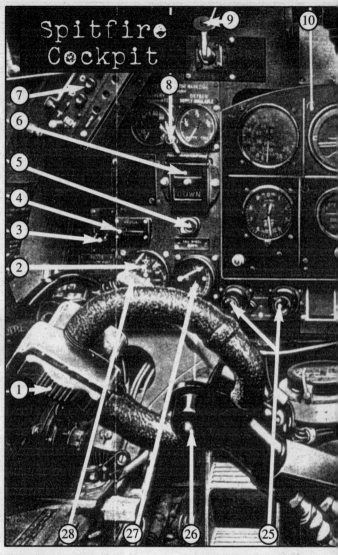

Spitfire Cockpit

1   Gun firing pushbutton
2   Pneumatic pressure gauge
3   Ignition switches
4   Undercarriage indicator master switch
5   Tailwheel indicator
6   Undercarriage indicator
7   Radio pushbutton controller

8   Oxygen regulator
9   Flap control
10   Instrument flying panel
11   Voltmeter
12   Engine speed indicator
13   Cockpit ventilator control
14   Supercharger override switch

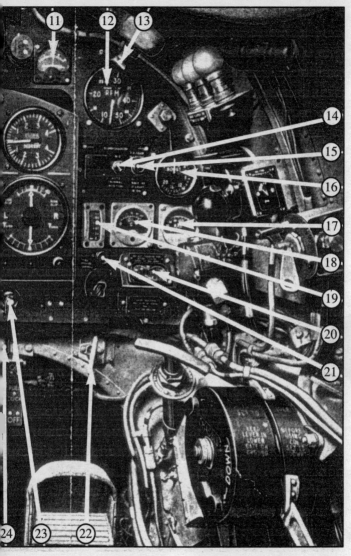

15 Supercharger warning light
16 Boost gauge
17 Coolant temperature gauge
18 Oil temperature gauge
19 Oil pressure gauge
20 Fuel contents gauge
21 Fuel pressure warning light

22 Starter breech reloading control
23 Engine starter pushbutton
24 Fuel cock control
25 Cockpit floodlight switches
26 Camera gun pushbutton
27 Elevator tab indicator
28 Brake lever

Pilot's
Kit List

Helmet — made of brown leather, with telephone earpieces in zipped padded oval housings. It had a chamois-leather lining, a chin strap and a slit back with adjustment strap, which acted as a quick-release to pull off the helmet and oxygen mask from the pilot's head in the event of baling out.

Goggles — a split-window mask made of celluloid with either a brass or Bakelite frame. Rubber padding surrounded the goggles.

Oxygen mask — fitted with an in-built microphone. Two types were in use during the Battle of Britain: Type C carbon microphone and Type 19 electro-magnetic microphone.

Gloves and gauntlets — inner gloves were made of silk and chamois, with woollen fingerless mitts over them, covered by brown leather outer gauntlets. Gloves were essential because warm hands were needed for careful flying and weapons use.

Flying boots — either the 1930 style, made of chestnut sheepskin with front zip fastening and a strap at the top; or the 1936 version: straight, pull-on, black leather with a fleecy lining and a tightening strap at the top.

Life jacket — 1932 version: a thick khaki, cotton-twill waistcoat closed with three buttons and two buckled straps, and housing a bladder (inflated by mouth). It was painted yellow to make the wearer more visible in the sea.

Leather flying jacket — usually tan in colour, done up with buttons, with large flapped pockets in the front.

Parachute — the canopy was made of silk up to 1943. Then it was made of white nylon. The harness was double-thickness, white cotton and linen webbing sewn together.

Commands and Airbases

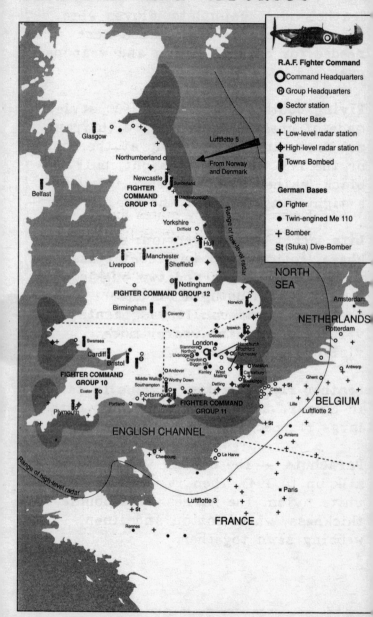

I was a pilot. My mates and I flew Spitfires in the Battle of Britain. I survived, but many of my friends did not. Much has been written and said about what happened during that fateful autumn, but this is what I saw with my own eyes.

John Smith, Spitfire pilot,
327 Squadron, 1940

Chapter 1
Under Attack

'Green Leader to Green Three, see anything yet?'

'Green Three to Green Leader. Nothing yet, skipper.'

'Radar says they're on their way. Keep 'em peeled.'

Green Three was me, John 'Bonzo' Smith. Nineteen years old. Third pilot in Green Section of 327 Squadron. Ian 'Tug' Banks was our skipper, the Section Leader. Charlie 'Dob' Masters was Green Two, the other pilot in our three-man section. 327 Squadron flew in three V-formations of three planes each: Red Section, Blue Section and Green Section.

We'd been scrambled from our base in Hornchurch, Essex, five minutes earlier, when our radar had warned that the Luftwaffe was on its way. Now we were flying over north Kent, just to the east of London. Below me I could see the mud flats of the Thames estuary, the river now wide and merging with the sea – cold and blue, so very different from the thin brown river that snaked through London.

'Still no sign.'

'Let's take a stroll and see what we can find,' came the voice of Jerry Payne, the leader of Red Section, in my headphones.

He took a turn to the right, and one by one each section followed him, spreading out so that we patrolled the east Kent area in a line formation.

I was relatively new to Spitfires. I'd joined 327 Squadron just two months earlier after my training, most of which had been done on Tiger Moths and Miles Masters. Compared to the Tiger and the Miles, the Spitfire was more cramped, but I soon learned the benefits of its slim design. The narrower Spitfire was able to turn much quicker and get you out of trouble when under attack. It was able to twist and turn, loop and dive in a short arc, providing you could take the strain that came with a sudden loss of gravity as you dived, or the increased pressure as you went into a steep climb. Even after two months I still felt excitement when at the controls of a Spitfire, surely the best fighter plane in the whole world!

Suddenly I saw the enemy planes approaching at 17,000 feet, about half a mile ahead of us: sixteen Messerschmitt Me-109s, instantly recognizable by their yellow nose-tips, flying in the German 'finger-four' formations.

'Here we go!' came Red Leader's voice over my headphones. 'Battle formations.'

'Green Section, line astern!' Tug ordered.

Dob and I brought our Spitfires into line behind Tug's plane. Then Tug dropped his nose and dived, while Dob and I soared up. As we'd hoped, the leading Me-109 went down after Tug, guns firing, but Tug had already hauled back hard on his controls and was now soaring upwards and banking to the right. The Me-109 pilot attempted to follow Tug, still shooting, but his flight path now brought him into my range. I kicked my rudder to the right, kept my gunsights ahead of him, turned the gun button to

'Fire' and let go with a three-second burst. The bullets from all of my eight guns hit him, raking the aircraft from nose to tail. A burst of flame shot upwards and the Me-109 spun away downwards, black smoke pouring from its engine.

'Bandits behind you, Green Three!' Dob shouted in my headphones.

I instinctively pushed the joystick forward and went into a dive, turning as I went. My plane shuddered as a burst of bullets tore into its fuselage. I pulled back hard into a steep climb and completed a loop which brought me on to the tail of my German opponent. He must have been expecting my move because he rolled to one side, just as I fired, and my bullets scraped past him.

'Better shooting next time, Bonzo!' Tug chuckled.

By now the sky was filled with thin lines of white smoke from planes as they looped and turned in the air. There were thicker lines of black smoke from those that had been hit.

I put my Spitfire into level flight and headed out towards the sea. Then I saw them ahead of me, emerging from the clouds: a fleet of Heinkel He-111 bombers with their Me-109 escorts flying in close formation at 13,000 feet. This was the real attack force; the first wave of Me-109s had come to clear the way for these bombers.

'Heinkels at twelve o'clock!' I barked into my microphone.

The rest of the squadron had already seen them and were quickly turning to attack.

Tug took his Spitfire to 14,000 feet, above the approaching He-111s. Dob and I followed him, flying now in a V-formation, keeping either side and just behind him. We flew over the first Heinkels, leaving them to Red Section, just behind us.

There was a chance that the new wave of Me-109s might break away and attack us. Luckily they remained close to their He-111s in their role as protectors, which meant their speed was limited to about 200 mph instead of their usual 330 mph.

'Going in!' said Tug's voice in my headphones.

He swooped down on the nearest Messerschmitt, his finger on the 'Fire' button. The German pilot pulled back into a climb to escape the stream of tracer bullets. Tug followed him, spiralling upwards. Now the right side of a Heinkel was left exposed for Dob to go in, guns blazing. The top machine-gunner saw him coming and let fly with both barrels. Dob swerved just in time to avoid his bullets and went into a dive, attempting to come up under the bomber. But the machine-gunner in the 'dustbin bay' beneath the plane started firing, trying to get a fix on him.

For a second, while both machine-gunners in the body of the He-111 were distracted, I had a chance, and I took it. I banked and came in fast just above the Heinkel, dropped my nose a fraction, and then let go with a two-second burst into the dome of the cockpit. I saw the glass shatter as my bullets tore into it before I had overtaken the plane. I turned sharply and headed straight back for it. The front of the Heinkel was a mess, its nose machine-gun out of action, but the pilot was still keeping on course. I managed to get another burst off and then abruptly changed course to fly along the top of the Heinkel. The bottom of my Spitfire barely missed the tip of the large bomber's tail fin.

I banked, preparing to come in for a third time, but there was no need. The He-111 was already diving out of control, flames flickering along the fuselage.

That's one Luftwaffe bomber that won't be doing any more damage, I thought to myself.

Suddenly I felt a massive *thump*, then an explosion knocked the controls out of my hands. The Spitfire dropped and the cockpit began to fill with smoke. Flames licked around my feet. As I plunged towards the ground I could feel myself starting to lose consciousness. The smoke had now filled the cockpit; I couldn't see anything or scarcely breathe. I didn't know if I was over land or sea; I didn't know my altitude; all I knew for certain was that I'd been hit and was trapped inside a burning plane.

I tried to force the cockpit hood back, but it was stuck. I knew I only had a few more seconds before either the smoke choked me or the plane smashed into the ground or the sea.

I undid my safety belt, lifted myself up and hit the hood with all my strength . . . and, as if by a miracle, this time it gave way and flew off. I grabbed the side of the cockpit and pushed myself out.

I fell through open sky for a few seconds before I pulled my rip-cord and the parachute opened above me. I looked down and the green fields below, previously so far away, rushed up to meet me.

I pulled on one side of the parachute, aiming clear of the line of trees that formed the boundary between two fields. I hit the ground and rolled over, then staggered back to my feet again as the parachute billowed down to the ground around me. Above me, the air battle still raged. I was alive . . .

'Put your hands up!' a voice behind me shouted. 'Make one false move and you're dead!'

Chapter 2
Landed

I raised my hands up and turned round to find myself face to face with a pitchfork. Behind it stood a large, elderly man dressed in farm labourer's clothes.

'Got you, you German spy.'

'German!' I gasped. Then I laughed. 'Do I look like or sound like a German?'

'Spies don't,' said the old man. 'But you can't fool me!'

There was the sound of running feet in a nearby field and a voice called out, 'Put that thing down, Joe, you idiot! He's one of ours!'

I saw another elderly man rush through a gap in a hedge. With him were two children, a boy and girl. They made their way over to me as I disentangled myself from my parachute. Joe lowered the pitchfork, but he still glared at me suspiciously.

The man who'd just arrived came up to me, shook my hand vigorously, beaming all the while. 'I'm sorry about that,' he said. 'Joe's been told so often to watch out for invading Germans that he's taken it a bit too seriously. My name's Josh Poole. This is my farm and these are my grandchildren, William and Carol. Are you OK?'

'Fine, thanks,' I said. 'Just a bit shaken up.'

The two children were still looking at me goggle-eyed, as if I was a man from outer space.

'I knew you were one of ours,' said William. 'I've got pictures of all the uniforms. That was a Spitfire you were flying, wasn't it?'

I nodded. 'Not much left of it now, though, I'm afraid,' I said ruefully.

'We'll talk later,' said Mr Poole. 'You'd better come up to the farmhouse and have a cup of tea. You'll feel better after that.'

'I need to get a message to my base and let them know I'm all right,' I said. 'Is there a telephone near here?'

'We've got one at the house,' said Mr Poole. 'And we'll see what the wife can rustle up for you in the way of food. I expect you're hungry after all that air-battling up there.'

'It's called dogfighting, Grandad,' explained William. 'Isn't it?' he said to me.

I nodded, and added with a grin, 'Though, frankly, most dogs are too clever to want to go up in a plane and do that sort of thing!'

We walked the mile or so across the fields to the Pooles' farmhouse. Now that Joe was convinced I wasn't a German, he insisted on carrying my parachute for me, despite my protests that I could carry it myself.

We got back to the farmhouse, where Mr Poole spent about five minutes trying to get hold of the operator. Finally I was able to get a message back to Hornchurch. I told them I was O K and would be back as soon as I could. Afterwards they sat me down at the table in the large warm kitchen and Mrs Poole handed me a huge plate of eggs and bacon and a big mug of steaming hot tea. I sat and ate hungrily, though it was hard to be completely relaxed because everyone was staring at me, in particular Joe and the two children. I must have been the first flyer they'd seen close up, and with all my gear on I must have cut an unusual figure for them.

'Have you been flying Spitfires long?' asked William, keen to find out more about his favourite plane.

'Where's Hornchurch?' asked Carol.

'Let the poor young man eat his meal,' said Mrs Poole.

'Too many questions,' muttered Joe darkly. 'Careless talk costs lives.'

'Joe's one of our keenest Home Guard members,' explained Mr Poole. 'He takes the orders he's given by our local captain very seriously.'

'Jerry won't invade while I'm around!' nodded Joe confidently.

As I ate I listened and got the picture: Mr Poole and Joe were both in the local unit of the Home Guard, Britain's last line of defence.

William and Carol were keen to talk about the war: how many German planes I'd shot down, did I think it would last long? – all those sorts of questions.

'I hope it goes on for a bit longer,' said William.

'That's a terrible thing to say, William,' said his grandmother. 'Think how many more people get killed every day it goes on.'

'Yes, but I want to fight, too,' said William, 'and I can't fight until I'm older.'

'With a bit of luck it'll all be over by Christmas,' said Mr Poole. 'If you ask me, Hitler's overstretched himself, rushing through Europe as fast as he did.'

'That's what they said last autumn,' said Mrs Poole soberly. 'They said it was all going to be over by last Christmas. If you ask me, this war'll go on and on. Just like the last one.'

'I'll do my best to make it as short as I can,' I threw in, trying to make as light of it as I could.

The clock on the mantelpiece chimed and I realized I'd been sitting here in this comfortable farmhouse, so near yet so far from the war, eating and chatting for an hour, and I suddenly felt guilty.

'I'd better be going,' I said. 'They'll be wondering what's taking me so long. If you could run me to the nearest station –'

'Run you to the station!' snorted Mr Poole. 'Nonsense! I'll run you back to your base.'

'But that's right on the other side of the Thames!' I protested.

'You're fighting for us, putting your life at risk every time you go up in one of those things,' said Mr Poole. 'The least I can do is take you back to your base. Anyway, how would you get your parachute back without me taking you, and that's vital to the war effort, that is.'

In the face of such determined kindness I could hardly refuse such an offer.

Mrs Poole had made me some sandwiches which she wrapped in greaseproof paper and pressed into my hand as I got into Mr Poole's old car. Mrs Poole, the two children and Joe waved us goodbye as we drove away.

As we headed north through the Kent countryside, Mr Poole explained to me why William was so keen to join up and fight.

'His dad, our son, Timmy, was killed at Dunkirk. It hit William especially hard.'

Then Mr Poole told me all about Timmy. What a good father he had been. A good farmer too, and a hard worker. How much the future had held for him. All I could do was to sit and listen and sympathize, and to promise that I would do my best to make sure that Timmy Poole hadn't died in vain.

By the time we got to Hornchurch darkness was starting to fall. Mr Poole let me off at the main gate. I struggled out of his car with my loosely packed parachute, shook him by the hand and told him that after the war was over I'd call on him again at his farm, and next time the meal would be on me! Mr Poole gave me a broad smile before driving off into the falling night.

The first person I ran into as I walked back into the base was Flight Sergeant 'Crusty' Pearson, so called because of his grumpy manner – always finding fault with everything and everyone.

'Mr Smith!' he barked. 'Where have you been? On holiday?'

'Kent, Flight,' I said. 'I did get a telephone message through. I was shot down and had to bale out.'

'I know you were shot down,' snapped Crusty. 'You nearly got yourself killed. That wouldn't have done at all.'

I was just starting to think that maybe Crusty had a warm heart underneath that tough exterior, when he spoilt it by adding,

'We can't afford to lose a trained pilot. Nor can we afford to lose fighters. You blokes are losing planes faster than we can replace them. You're in trouble, sir!'

Just my luck! I groaned to myself. Not only do I nearly get myself killed, now I'm going to be court-martialled for destroying RAF property!

Chapter 3

Missing in Action

As Crusty glowered at me, I decided I wasn't going to go down without a fight.

'I did shoot down two of theirs, Flight,' I pointed out. 'Two for the price of one, so we showed a profit!'

'We need a ratio of six to one to make a profit; five to one to break even,' snapped Crusty. 'We're outnumbered, remember?'

Tug Banks and Dob Masters had been watching this exchange and they came over to greet me as Crusty marched off.

When side by side, Tug and Dob always reminded me of Laurel and Hardy. Tug was small, thin and wiry, while Dob was tall and wide. Dob even had a moustache, small at the moment but one that he was growing into a handlebar style.

'Return of the wandering hero,' grinned Tug.

'How dare you upset poor kind-hearted Flight Sergeant Pearson!' added Dob with a broad smile. 'He only has your welfare at heart.'

'Huh! To hear him talk, anyone would think they were his own private planes,' I said, still feeling a bit sour about the way Crusty had told me off.

'Don't mind him, Bonzo,' said Tug. 'He's like that with everyone. I wrecked the first plane I ever took out, never even got it off the ground. Put down the nose too sharply as I was taking off and somersaulted.' Tug laughed. 'So next time Crusty moans at you if you lose a plane, tell him at least you got it off the ground, which was more than your section leader did.'

'I don't intend to lose any more,' I said confidently. 'At least, not if I can help it.'

'We're off to the Mess for a cup of tea,' said Dob. 'Come and join us, but pick up your post first. There are a couple of letters for you.'

They headed off for the Mess, while I hurried to the post boxes in the Operations hut.

As Dob had said, there were two letters waiting for me. One was from my mother; I recognized her very tight handwriting on the envelope. The other was from my elder brother, Edward, which was the one I opened first. Edward was fighting overseas and I was keen to hear how he was getting on.

Like the military man he was, Edward's letter gave nothing away, not even whereabouts in the world he was. For all anyone else who read the letter could tell, Edward could have been in Africa or South America, although the word in the family was that he and his unit had been sent to Norway.

The letter had been written some weeks ago. As always, Edward's tone was cheerful, full of funny anecdotes about the trouble he had with finding boot laces to fit and wondering if a steel helmet was really that much defence if a bomb dropped directly on you. That was Edward's way, always making a joke of things. He ended, *Have you heard anything from Ma and Pa? If you see them give them my love. I've dropped them a note, too, but with this war you never know if any of these letters are actually get-ting through.*

Next, I opened the letter from my mother. It was very short, not much news. They hadn't heard from Edward – though I guessed they would have by now. Father was well, though his leg was giving him trouble. They looked forward to seeing me when I got a chance for a spot of leave.

As luck would have it I was due for leave, and when I got to the Mess to join Tug and Dob, Tug suggested I take it the next day.

'After all, we haven't got a plane for you at the moment. With a bit of luck your replacement kite should be here the day after tomorrow, so you might as well take tomorrow off and see your folks. The way Hitler's stepping up his air attacks there's no knowing when you'll get the chance for leave next.'

Taking Tug's advice, I arranged a leave pass and next morning set off for my parents' house in London. I got a lift to the station and travelled up to London by train. I needed the time on the train to think, to prepare myself for the ordeal of a visit. That sounds a terrible thing to say when talking about your own parents, but the truth was my father had disapproved of my joining the RAF. Pa had been a colonel in the Fusiliers in the First World War. That was when he'd received the injury to his leg, which kept him out of active service during this war. His father, my grandfather, had been in the same regiment, as had my great-grandfather before him. My father had always expected me to follow Edward and join the Fusiliers – the 'family regiment', as Pa called it. We'd been a family of professional army men for generations – soldiers to the last. Instead I'd joined the RAF.

While at Oxford, I'd joined the University Air Squadron, the pleasure of flying being second to none, as far as I was concerned. When war was declared it seemed a natural progression for me to volunteer for the RAF. For Pa this was a blow he found hard to take. He didn't understand planes. For him war was guns and barbed wire, bayonets and tanks – soldiers' work. Although he didn't say it as such, I sensed that he thought 'fly boys', as he called pilots, were cowards who couldn't confront the enemy face to face like soldiers had to. What with that – and his feeling that I'd betrayed him by not joining the family regiment, as Edward had done – our meetings had become tense. Not that things had been that easy between Pa and myself before, anyway.

Whether it was bitterness that he had been invalided out of the army, or that he just wasn't the kind of man who liked children much, even his sons, I never found out. All I did know was, once Edward and I had stopped being infants, Pa had been difficult to make conversation with. There was something very reserved about him. And very angry. I wasn't looking forward to seeing him again and maybe getting into another argument with him. Still, I wasn't only going home to see him, I was going to see Ma and see how she was bearing up.

Our family home was near Regent's Park, in the centre of London, walking distance from everywhere, as Pa said. It was one of those large old houses with bow windows at the front. Just like the Fusiliers had been handed down from father to son, so had the house. It was a family heirloom and would be handed on to Edward when Pa died, though Edward had always told me he didn't really want it. Edward wanted to live in the countryside where he could ride and shoot and fish. He once said the only things he could shoot from this house were the animals in Regent's Park Zoo.

When I arrived home I realized that Ma wasn't bearing up too well. Although she forced a smile and gave me a hug, I could see that she'd been crying.

'What on earth's the matter?' I asked her.

'It's Edward,' said my father from behind her as he came into the hall from his study.

'Edward?' I asked, puzzled. Then I laughed and gave Ma a hug. 'If you're worried because you haven't heard from him, don't be. I had a letter from him only yesterday. He's fine, but he did say he wondered if you'd got his letters.'

'We've heard,' said my mother.

She moved away from me and went to the hall table. She picked up a telegram and gave it to me. 'This arrived this morning,' she said.

The words were very stark and simple: *Regret to inform your son Edward Smith missing in action.*

I put the telegram back on the table. I didn't know what to say. Edward. Missing in action. That usually only meant one thing: dead, but we're afraid we can't find his body. I felt numb, a cold sort of anger. Edward – the joker, so full of life, always at the heart of any party – lying dead out there somewhere, presumably in the snows of Norway.

I put my arm around Ma and forced a smile.

'All that means is he's missing,' I said, trying to cheer her up. 'He could have been taken prisoner and the other side are taking their time about letting us know. Or he might have escaped, be hiding out some-where, unable to get in touch.' I forced another smile. Like the first, it was one I didn't really feel. 'Edward'll be all right, I'm sure of it. Look at the scrapes he used to get into when we were boys, but he always came up smiling. He'll turn up safe and sound, you'll see!'

But my words sounded hollow even to me.

The rest of that day was dismal. Ma tried to be cheerful for my sake, chatting about what the neighbours were up to, who was joining up with which regiment, who was getting married. Pa didn't say much. He never said much at the best of times; now with Edward missing, he was even more quiet than usual.

At least it meant he didn't start criticizing me or the RAF, so we never got into a row. However, I was glad when it was time for me to return to Hornchurch.

The streets of London were in darkness as I headed back to base. Black-out time: all the windows covered, all vehicles with their headlights hooded. With my brother missing, presumed dead, and the Germans just across the Channel, poised to invade, it was a dark time in more ways than one.

Chapter 4

Dogfight After Dogfight

Back at my squadron I was presented with my new Spitfire by Crusty with the warning words, 'Take good care of this one.'

Early the next morning I sat out in the warm sunshine with the rest of 327 Squadron and 58 Squadron and waited to be sent up. We sat around in deck-chairs, on wooden crates, on anything we could find in fact. Tug Banks had even discovered an old armchair from somewhere and had dumped it outside the Operations hut. He now reclined in it in comfort and luxury. I made do with one of the rickety deck-chairs. All of us wore our flying gear, complete with helmets, ready and waiting. When the call came there was no time to waste getting ready: it was run to the plane and get airborne as fast as possible.

'Maybe they won't come today,' murmured Dob, who was sitting next to me on a battered wooden crate. 'Not after what we did to them yesterday.'

'Oh?' I asked, intrigued. 'What happened yesterday?'

'Well, young Bonzo,' grinned Tug, 'while you were enjoying the delights of London, some of us were heavily engaged in trying to defeat the enemy.'

I hadn't told them about Edward going missing, so Dob and Tug just assumed I'd spent the day relaxing with my parents. And although they knew from things I'd said that my father disapproved of my going into the RAF, I hadn't let on how deep his hurt and anger went, so there was no way for them to know that my day's leave hadn't been a day of enjoyment but one of sadness and misery.

'Yesterday was a triumph of co-operation,' put in Dob. 'Eleven Group and Ten Group working together with pretty spectacular results.'

(Here at Hornchurch we were part of Fighter Command's 11 Group, which covered the south-east of England. While 10 Group, to the west of us, looked after Dorset, Somerset and the rest of the south-west.)

Apparently radar had picked up a large number of German planes coming in to attack a shipping convoy.

'Reports say that only four of the ships made it to port out of the original convoy of twenty,' grunted Tug. 'Sixteen ships lost. But the Jerries paid dearly for it. We hit them hard. By the end of it we reckon they'd lost sixty planes to our nineteen. It might make them have second thoughts about attacking again today.'

As if to prove him wrong, at that moment the bell sounded. Immediately we all leapt up and began to run towards our planes. Over the loudspeaker came the voice of the Sector Controller: '327 Squadron take off and patrol base. Further information in the air.'

I climbed on to the wing and clambered into the cockpit of my Spitfire. Starting my engine, I began my run over the grass, using the brakes and throttle to swing the plane from side to side. The Spitfire's long nose made forward vision almost impossible. It was wonderful in the air but on the ground the machine was difficult to handle, and as a result more than one pilot had crashed his plane even before take off.

I aimed the Spitfire at the boundary of the airfield, turning its nose gently into the wind, and opened up the throttle to four pounds of boost. The Spitfire had great acceleration. I pushed the stick forward to lift the tail and get a good airflow over the elevators, and became airborne almost at once, soaring into the sky. Pulling the control column back, I set the throttle for a good climbing speed of 200 mph. Now safely aloft, I slid the Perspex hood of the cockpit shut.

Dob and I slotted ourselves into our V-formation, to one side of and just behind Tug's leading plane. We reached 15,000 feet and levelled out. As we flew, every plane in the formation – the whole squadron – weaved from side to side to make it easier to see the enemy. If one of us spotted anything we alerted all the others straight away.

Over the radio came the voice of the Controller: 'Hello, Red Leader.' Our squadron leader, Jerry Payne, was Red Leader, right at the front. As always, Blue and Green Sections were just behind.

'Reading you, Control,' came Payne's voice.

'Bandits at twenty thousand, coming at you on a direct interception course.'

'Read that, Control,' Payne responded. 'OK, chaps,' he said to us, 'all sections up to twenty-three thousand. Let's hit them from above and give them a surprise.'

This time the German force was a mixture of Dornier bombers, Junkers Ju-87s (Stuka dive-bombers) and Messerschmitt Me-109s. As always the Me-109s were riding shotgun for the bombers. After all, the aim of the German raids was to bomb Britain into submission, so the bombers were our main targets, not the fighters. But to get to the Dorniers we had to get past the Me-109s.

Battle started at once. Red Section swooped down into the attack, Blue following, with our Green Section behind them. Within seconds the air was a mass of fighter planes soaring, wheeling and leaving white trails of criss-crossed smoke. The large

Dorniers kept on a steady course while we flew at them, hitting them when and where we could. The Stukas were more manoeuvrable than the Dorniers and some took evasive action.

While Tug engaged an Me-109 escort in a dogfight, Dob and I went for the nearest Dornier. He let it have a burst of tracer into its nose, while I went for its tail plane. Without one, any plane was as good as dead.

My burst smashed into the Dornier's rear, blowing away its rudder and ripping holes in the rear elevators. The bomber lurched in the sky, then Dob came round again and let off another burst into its rear end that finished it off. The Dornier began to plunge earthwards and, as we watched, we saw the crew leap out one after the other, their parachutes opening and billowing out white. But there was no time to admire our handiwork because now we were under attack from Me-109s.

The aerial battle went on for about twenty minutes, although it seemed much longer. The surviving Dorniers dropped their bomb loads before turning back to the coast. The Stukas did the same. I got one of them as it came back up after its bombing run, my tracer bullets raking completely along its side. I felt a sense of satisfaction as black smoke billowed out from its engine. It went into a dive from which I knew it wouldn't recover. That was one Stuka that wouldn't be dive-bombing again.

As the surviving bombers and fighter planes headed out to sea, we gave chase, but not for long.

'Back to base, squadron,' Red Leader's voice came over my radio. 'Save some fuel for next time.'

He was right, of course. More than one over-keen pilot had given chase to retreating enemy planes, only to find himself over the sea with the red light winking to tell him he was out of fuel. Ditching in the Channel wasn't an experience I fancied. Planes tended to sink very fast once they hit the water. And the chances of being picked up by British boats became that much slimmer the further you were from the shore.

I turned my plane and followed the rest of the squadron back across the Kent countryside to Essex. We came in to land

and taxied over towards the Operations hut. As we did I counted the planes. Twelve of us had gone up. Ten had come back. I hoped our two missing pilots had had the same luck that I'd had: that they'd been able to bale out and were perhaps now eating bacon and eggs and drinking tea in some friendly farmer's kitchen.

As we walked over to the Mess I joined up with Dob Masters. 'Any idea who didn't make it back?'

'I saw Proctor bale out early on,' said Dob. 'I'm pretty sure he's safe. I'm not so sure about Squires, though.'

Walter Squires was a very courageous pilot with Red Section. He had taught me a lot when I first joined the squadron. Defence was his strong point. 'Always look for a way out before you go in' was his motto. It looked as if this time he hadn't been lucky enough to find a way out.

We had barely been in the Mess for ten minutes, drinking a welcome cup of tea, when the bell to scramble us went.

'Not again!' said Tug. 'Don't those Germans have anything better to do?'

It went on like this for the next ten days.

It was the heaviest concentration of attacks we'd experienced so far. Six or seven times a day the bell sounded to send us up, and into the air we went, fighting dogfight after dogfight with the Germans, shooting their planes down and watching them shoot our planes down. Still they kept coming. Throughout the day. Attack after attack. Often when we came back there was someone missing. Familiar faces no longer there, to be replaced by new ones straight out of training. But there weren't enough pilots left in training to fill the gaps that were appearing. It was the same at every airbase across England. New squadrons had to be made up with Polish pilots, Czech ones, Canadians or New Zealanders. Different backgrounds, different languages, but the same aim: to defend Britain.

It seemed like there was never a minute when we weren't either up there fighting the Luftwaffe or waiting for it to attack. After a week of this some of the lads were so tired that they didn't even bother to get out of their planes after landing. They just taxied to a space on the field, switched off the engine and fell asleep in their cockpit.

On the tenth morning, 14 August, I woke up after about an hour's sleep – although it seemed like only a few minutes – as dawn was breaking. The sky was clear. Peaceful.

I stepped outside the hut and stood, looking out over the airfield and thinking how quiet it was, how very English, with the red sun coming up through the trees that bordered the eastern side of the airfield. It was a perfect August morning. Dob joined me.

'Jerry's late today,' he said.

'Their alarm clocks can't have gone off,' I joked.

We wandered over to our chairs on the grass and sat down to admire the sunrise.

'Maybe they've given up?' said Dob.

'Ssssh!' I chortled. 'You said that before, and look what happened!'

'Yes, but they can't have that many planes left after the last three days,' Dob pointed out. 'We must have shot down hundreds of them. Not just us here, but everyone else.'

'We've lost planes too,' I pointed out. 'In fact, sometimes I think that the winner of this will be the side that has the last plane left flying.'

We sat there, watching the sun slowly rise, hearing the birds singing in the trees as it appeared.

'At least we've got radar,' sighed Dob.

I nodded. There was no doubt that our radar had given us the edge in this battle so far. The whole of the south coast and parts of the east coast of England were dotted with radar stations. They could give us good advance warning of an attack. The Luftwaffe had tried to bomb the radar stations but, luckily, so far it had had little effect. Some of the tall radar masts had been destroyed and the receiver huts damaged, but thanks to the large number of radar stations the early-warning system had been able to keep going. At least, that was what I thought on that August morning, sitting there in the warm early morning sun with Dob Masters.

The bell sounded. Scramble. Thanks to the radar, we had about five minutes to get to our planes and off the ground – time enough to be there on an intercept course. Only today we didn't have five minutes. We didn't even have five seconds. As Dob and I stood up, we heard them. The drones of the engines of heavy German bombers. Then we saw them, at the same time as we heard the Controller's voice over the loudspeaker: 'Enemy bombing formation approaching! Take cover immediately!'

'They must have knocked out our radar!' gasped Dob.

As we looked up the first bomb came screaming directly towards us.

Chapter 5
Bombed!

'Down!' I yelled, and I threw myself at Dob. We both crashed to the grass as the bomb whistled over our heads. Seconds later it exploded only about two hundred yards away. A shower of stones and earth cascaded down on us. I rolled over and glanced behind me. A huge smouldering crater had been blown into the ground. Dob and I looked up as we heard the Stukas coming back.

'Shelter!' I shouted, and we both ran for the nearest one. As we did so we heard a bomber's machine-guns open fire and bullets began to rip into the ground behind us. I threw myself through the entrance of the bomb shelter and tumbled down the concrete steps into it. Dob did likewise, landing on top of me.

Six other people were already there: two pilots and four ground crew. Dob and I picked ourselves up from the hard floor and shook dirt and cement off our clothes. Smoke and dust billowed down into the shelter as the bombs dropped on the base. With each fresh explosion the building shuddered and then settle down again.

The Luftwaffe must have knocked out some of our radar positions to have got this far without us being warned. With the radar gone, that left only the manned observation posts dotted around, and by the time they could get a warning to the airbases the enemy was on target – as we had just found out to our cost. I wondered what the damage was like outside. How many planes had the German bombers destroyed? What shape was the airfield in?

The bombing raid seemed to go on for ever, though it must have only lasted for about five minutes. When at last we heard the sound of the All Clear we emerged from the shelter.

The airfield was a mess. Three Spitfires had been completely destroyed. Another two planes had been badly shot up: there were gaping holes in their cockpit hoods and fuselages, as well as wings hanging loose. One of the buildings had taken a direct hit and was now just a smouldering pile of bricks and rubble. One of the runways had two deep craters in it. Fortunately the other runways had only suffered minor damage.

Dob and I wandered out across the airfield, inspecting the aftermath of the attack. We knew that other airfields had been badly bombed, but it was the first time either of us had experienced it here at Hornchurch.

'What a mess!' groaned Dob.

'Attention!' came the Sector Controller's voice over the loudspeakers. 'Station commander's orders: Every available man and woman to report to Operations and collect a shovel or other tools. All holes to be filled in as priority.'

Dob and I hurried along with everyone else – pilots, canteen staff, radio operators, clerks – to collect our tools. We were lucky the Germans didn't return for a further attack. It was my guess that they thought they'd put Hornchurch out of action for good, so they were turning on other bases.

Luckily they'd underestimated the determination of everybody on the airbase to get Hornchurch active again.

For the next few hours we slaved away, muscles aching as we shovelled earth into wheelbarrows and dumped it back into the craters, gradually filling them up. After two hours of this, those of us who weren't used to so much physical labour were ready to take to our beds and get some rest, but we knew that time was short. We had to get the base back into operation.

By the end of the afternoon every hole was repaired, with the exception of the two giant craters in the main runway, which would take a little longer to fill. The main thing was that the airfield was operational again.

We'd just finished filling in the holes and were looking forward to going to the Mess and giving our tired limbs a rest, when the bell sounded.

'Scramble!' came the Controller's voice. 'Bandits coming in from the east!'

'Already!' groaned Dob.

And so we were off again on a sortie.

*

As it turned out, our radar system hadn't been knocked out completely, just a few of the masts. By extending the range of the surviving radar positions while they were being repaired, our coastal early-warning system was soon functional again.

We went up again that evening just to show the Luftwaffe that it hadn't put us out of business. Our squadron bagged two of its bombers and two fighters for the loss of just one of our planes.

Just when we thought it couldn't get any worse, it did. The next day, 15 August, brought the biggest German attack so far.

Time and time again we went up into the air as wave after wave of Luftwaffe bombers and fighters poured over. By late afternoon we were all at the point of exhaustion. When you get that tired your concentration starts to go, and when you're flying at 350 mph against crack opposition who are determined to kill you, you need every ounce of your concentration if you are to survive.

Maybe it was the exhaustion, maybe the feeling that he'd come through dogfights so many times that he was invincible, whatever it was, Dob Masters was shot down at dusk. He and I were coming in to attack a Heinkel bomber and one of its machine-gunners hit Dob's plane with tracer that tore off his propeller. I didn't know if the bullets had hit Dob himself, all I saw in that split second was his plane go into an abrupt dive, spinning as it dropped, wings whirling round like a windmill. In situations like this there is a danger of 'redding out'. This can happen when a pilot changes direction too quickly or goes into sudden dive, pushing blood up into his brain. Then all you can see is red, literally. Nothing else. I just hoped Dob had had time to bale out before he had become blind.

I was determined to pay the Heinkel back for hitting Dob. I came at the bomber from the front and placed a burst of bullets into its nose and carried it on right along the length of the fuselage. Then I climbed, did a turn and a loop and came back for my second run at it. That was my mistake. I should have remembered Walter Squires's advice: 'Always look for a way out.' Instead I was so determined to down the Heinkel that I didn't see the Me-109 coming at me from behind. The first I knew about it was an enormous *thump* from my port side that seemed to knock my plane sideways, and then I was dropping out of the sky.

I managed to bring the Spitfire under control and levelled out. Next I tried to climb, only the plane wouldn't respond. So I looked out at my port wing and realized that it had been badly hit: there were gaping holes all over it. I could even see parts of the Browning machine-guns in the wing, buckled and bent. With only one good wing, it was going to be touch and go whether I got back to base safely.

I managed to turn and set a course for home. The plane was veering to one side and rocking and bucking like a mad horse. I held on like grim death to the joystick to prevent it from going round in circles. The struggle continued all the way back to Essex. I was determined to keep that rash promise I'd made to Crusty Pearson that I wasn't going to give him the pleasure of reprimanding me for losing any more planes. I'd bring this one back no matter what state it was in. The nearer I got to base the harder it was to keep the Spitfire in the air.

Soon I could see the runway of Hornchurch just ahead. Judging my approach, I brought the crippled plane in on as straight a line as I could, struggling against a strong side wind. With the engine roaring, I wobbled in, going all over the place.

I hit the ground with a tremendous thud, bounced up and then came down again. I pulled up near the Operations hut, from where Crusty Pearson appeared as I stepped down from my bullet-strafed cockpit.

'There you are, Flight,' I said, gesturing at the ruined wing. 'I said I'd bring the next one back.'

I waited for the rest of the squadron to return, hoping they would have news of Dob, but there was none. He didn't come home.

Chapter 6
The New Pilot

Dob's replacement arrived two days later. Gordon McBurn, a nineteen-year-old Kiwi. He was a bit shorter than me, about five feet eight, with a mass of ginger hair. He'd been training here for the past two months, having come over to 'do my bit for the old country', as he called it. His family had originally gone to New Zealand from Scotland just before he was born. With a name like McBurn, it seemed natural that we nicknamed him Scotty.

I now moved up to Green Two, taking Dob's place as first wing man to our section leader, while Scotty took over from me as Green Three.

That first morning when Scotty joined our squadron, Tug Banks left it to me to look after him and fill him in on how things worked, while Tug made some adjustments to his plane. Luckily for us the Luftwaffe was late that morning: fog over the Channel had given us a well-needed, few hours' respite.

I learnt that Scotty had joined the Royal New Zealand Air Force (RNZAF) when he was eighteen and a half, the youngest age at which he could sign up.

'The way a lot of us in New Zealand see it,' said Scotty, 'is that if Britain falls, then all of us out in New Zealand are going to end up as part of the German Reich. It wouldn't be long before we had German troops jackbooting through Christchurch and Wellington. There's no way we're going to let that happen if we can help it.'

He told me there were about a hundred Kiwis like him who'd come out to fly with the RAF and defend the country that was the hub of the British Empire. Scotty's training in New Zealand had mainly been in Tiger Moths. The first time he'd been in a Spitfire had been six weeks ago. Now here he was, about to go into battle against hardened and experienced Luftwaffe pilots. As I looked at him, sitting there in his flying gear, I thought that he seemed so much younger than me, even though we were the same age. I'd seen my comrades die and narrowly escaped death myself. I'd shot and killed other human beings. As I looked at him, I felt a sudden wave of sadness.

So often it was the newest pilots who died, frequently during their first battle. They didn't have the experience of fighting in the sky and hadn't yet developed that sixth sense that comes from being in dogfight after dogfight, that heightened sensation when you know that someone is on your tail, or has you in their gunsights, and you abruptly change course. If a new fighter pilot could survive his first encounter with the enemy, then he had a chance of surviving the next. I decided to pass on some tips to Scotty that I'd picked up in the hope that they would keep him alive, at least during his first fight.

'When we go up, do exactly what Tug Banks says,' I told him. 'He's our section leader and he's survived longer than any of us. Trust him. If he says fly head on at them, then fly head on at them. He knows what he's doing.

'The next thing to remember is: when you're up there on your own, forget all the fancy stuff – going into a tight spin or looping the perfect loop and all that clever stuff. It's OK in a flying circus, but it also fixes your line of flight for the opposition, and the more time they've got to get a good fix on your flightpath, the easier it is for them to shoot you down. Keep them guessing about the direction you're going next.

'Come at them out of the sun if it's possible. That'll blind them. And watch out for them trying to turn you into the sun. They'll do it if they can.

'Remember, our job is to hit the bombers. If we knock one of their fighters down it's a bonus, but it's the bombers that are doing the damage to our airfields and cities. When you attack a bomber, aim for the cockpit. Knock out the pilot and the plane goes down. That means hitting it from the front. The only trouble with that is that the machine-gunner in the cockpit will have you as a direct target. Another way is to hit the bomber's tailplane, but you have to hit it very hard to blow it away, and those German bombers are damn well made.

'I've found the best and safest way is to hit a plane directly from behind. If you're lucky the tailplane hides you from view as you come in.

'When you're shooting, remember always to fire ahead of the enemy plane. You've got to allow for its speed. Fire just before it gets into your gunsights. Unless you're coming at it dead ahead or from dead behind, of course.

'In battle, try to avoid shadowing any of your own wing men too closely. Two planes flying together in close formation are an easier target to hit than two planes flying erratically all over the sky. Often it's the second plane that gets it because the enemy has used the first plane as a marker.

'Remember that the enemy is no different from you. He's as scared as you. His plane is no better than yours. And in the case of the Luftwaffe fighter pilots, he has to remain with his bombers. He's not supposed to fly all over the sky; he has to stay put, which makes him a better target.'

Finally, more as a reminder to myself, I said ruefully, 'And don't take chances. Before you go in, look for the way out.'

Scotty didn't have much time to think about this advice, because just then the Controller's voice came over the speakers: '327 Squadron, Blue and Green Sections. Scramble!'

The next second we were running to our planes. I gave Scotty a thumbs-up sign as he clambered into his Spitfire. Helmets on, engines starting up, parachutes and safety harnesses fastened, chocks away, and then we were off, across the grass and up into the air.

Scrambling only one or two sections of a squadron had become standard practice with 11 Group. Done on a rota basis, it gave the pilots a little more rest. The other sections could be sent up if needed. They were also there in reserve if the enemy suddenly came with a second attack from another direction.

'Control to sections. Course one twenty and climb to fifteen thousand,' came the voice over our headphones.

I turned on to a heading of 120 degrees and followed Tug as we went into our climb. I looked across at Scotty in Green Three. He flew well, maintaining his position level and parallel with mine, behind and just above Tug's plane. The altimeter needle moved round as we climbed up into clouds. We were quickly through them into the clear blue sky above.

Once again we heard Control's voice on the radio: 'Green Section. Control calling. Bandits approaching you from the east at fourteen thousand. Continue on present course. Over to you.'

'Read that, Control,' we heard Tug answer. 'OK, chaps, tally-ho.'

Scotty and I followed Tug in a straight line, skimming the tops of the clouds, keeping our eyes peeled for the approaching German planes. According to Control they should be 1,000 feet below us, within the belt of cloud.

'Down we go, chaps,' came Tug's voice.

We followed him as he made a shallow dive into the thick cloud. Somewhere within it were our enemy, but whether they were ahead or behind us, we couldn't tell.

Suddenly we were in a break in the clouds and heading straight towards us were two Dorniers, in line-astern formation, with their Me-109 escorts.

'Fire!' yelled Tug.

We all three pressed our gun buttons at once. We must have caught the Germans by surprise, coming so suddenly out of the clouds in front of them. Our bullets smashed into the front of the first Dornier. We barely had time to register that it was on its way down, with thick black smoke pouring from its shattered nose, before we were almost on the second one. The Me-109s moved to defend their bomber.

Tug and I took out the leading Me-109s, pouring lead into them as they came for us, although bullets from one of them tore through my cockpit just above my head. Then we soared away.

Out of the corner of my eye I saw that Scotty was still with us, keeping close, as I'd told him to. I hoped he'd also remembered my bit of advice about separating once the dogfight really got under way, otherwise he could find himself in real trouble.

Tug swooped down towards the surviving Dornier, and as he did so its top machine-gunner opened up, forcing him to swing away.

I saw the Dornier's bomb load leave its belly, long sticks in a falling line. I managed to get off a burst from my machine-guns, but the Dornier turned in an arc and my tracer went harmlessly past its nose.

The Me-109s were also beginning their turn and heading back home. They hadn't been scared off; they were just low on fuel.

We gave chase for a few moments, just long enough to make sure they were definitely leaving, then Tug said: 'OK, chaps, home. Don't waste fuel and ammo. They'll be needed next time.'

The three of us turned and began our return flight to Hornchurch, still keeping alert in case one of the Me-109s should change its mind and decide to attack us from the rear. One Dornier and two Me-109s down for no loss to our side. Even Flight Sergeant Crusty Pearson should be satisfied with that.

Twenty minutes later we touched down on the grass one after the other, Tug first, then me, then Scotty.

Tug and I caught up with Scotty as he clambered down from the cockpit of his plane. He took his helmet and goggles off, and the expression on his face looked shaken, but at the same time exhilarated.

'Well done, young 'un,' Tug said to him. 'Keep flying like that and we might have a Section that stays together. I'll see you both in the Mess.'

Scotty smiled as Tug walked off to the Control hut to report in. 'I don't think I've ever been so scared as just before we went in for that first attack,' he said.

'It was the same for all of us,' I said. 'It's one thing flying for fun, it's entirely another when someone up there is trying to kill you.'

'But once it started I didn't feel scared any more,' he said. 'Even though it got worse, bullets flying around.'

'I know,' I said. 'It's strange. It's like some animal instinct for survival takes over. You don't think, you just act.'

I patted him on the shoulder.

'Well done, Scotty. You're one of us now.'

BATTLE OF BRITAIN AIRCRAFT

RAF Aircraft

Vickers Supermarine Spitfire 1A
single-seat fighter

Specification
Engine: One Rolls-Royce Merlin III 12-cylinder V,
1,030 hp at take-off
Armament: Eight 0.303-inch (0.77 cm) Browning
machine-guns with 300 rounds per gun
Speed: 365 mph (587 kmph) at 19,000 feet (5,790 m)
Climb: 9 minutes 24 seconds to 20,000 feet (6,095 m)
Ceiling: 34,000 feet (10,362 m)
Range: 575 miles (925 km)
Weight: 4,860 lb (2,204 kg) (empty);
        6,200 lb (2,812 kg) (loaded)
Span: 32 feet 10 inches (9.39 m)
Length: 29 feet 11 inches (9.06 m)
Height: 12 feet 7 inches (3.83 m)

The Supermarine Spitfire was the most agile plane
flown in the Battle of Britain. It could even
outmanoeuvre the Messerschmitt Me-109E. Another
element that gave the Spitfire its superiority was
its eight wing-mounted Browning machine-guns.
Even though they were out-ranged by the German
cannon, they had a decisive concentration of
rounds per second.

Hawker Hurricane single-seat fighter

Specification
Engine: One Rolls-Royce Merlin III
12-cylinder V, 1,030 hp at take-off
Armament: Eight 0.303-inch (0.77 cm) Browning
machine-guns with 334 rounds per gun
Speed: 324 mph (521 kmph) at 16,250 feet (4,952 m)
Climb: 8 minutes 30 seconds to 20,000 feet (6,095 m)
Ceiling: 34,200 feet (10,424 m)
Range: 505 miles (812 km)
Weight: 4,982 lb (2,259 kg)(empty);
        6,447 lb (2,924 kg) (loaded)
Span: 40 feet (12 m)
Length: 31 feet 4 inches (9.55 m)
Height: 13 feet 1 inch (3.98 m)

The Hurricane was Britain's first monoplane
fighter. Although it was later replaced by the
Spitfire, many fighter pilots who flew aerial
combat in both planes preferred the Hurricane
because the sloping nose gave better forward vision
than the long nose of the Spitfire. The pilots also
liked its robust build, which made it solid and
reliable and able to take a lot of punishment. With
a more sturdy and wider undercarriage than the
Spitfire, it was also easier to land.

Luftwaffe Aircraft

Messerschmitt Bf109 E3
single-seat fighter

Specification

Engine: One Daimler-Benz DB 601Aa 12-cylinder V inline, 1,175 hp at take-off

Armament: Two 20-mm MG FF cannon with 60 rounds per gun in the wings; two 7.9-mm MG17 machine-guns with 1,000 rounds (600 when MG FF/M installed) per gun in the fuselage, and one optional 20-mm MG FF/M with 200 rounds in the nose

Speed: 348 mph (560 kmph) at 14,560 feet (4,437 m)

Climb: 7 minutes 45 seconds to 19,685 feet (5,999 m)

Ceiling: 34,450 feet (10,500 m)

Range: 410 miles (659 m)

Weight: 4,189 lb (1,900 kg) (empty);
      5,875 lb (2,664 kg) (loaded)

Span: 32 feet 4 inches (9.86 m)

Length: 28 feet 4 inches (8.63 m)

Height: 8 feet 2 inches (2.49 m)

This plane was known as the 'Emil' to its pilots. It was as fast as the Spitfire, although not as manoeuvrable. The Me-109 had the ability to outdive both the Hurricane and the Spitfire. Crucially, its 20-mm guns fired at a slower rate than either of its two opposing British fighter planes. Despite its greater armament power, it actually demanded more skill to achieve decisive damage.

Heinkel He-111 H16 medium bomber

Specification

Engines: Two Junkers Jumo 211F-2 inverted-V piston engines, 1,350 hp each at take-off

Armament: In the nose: one 20-mm MG FF trainable, forward-firing cannon with 180 rounds; one optional 7.92 mm. MG15 trainable, forward-firing machine-gun. Dorsal position: one 13-mm MG131 trainable, rearward-firing machine-gun with 1,000 rounds; two 7.92-mm MG81 rearward-firing machine-guns with 1,000 rounds per gun; one 7.92 MG15; one MG81 lateral-firing machine-gun with 1,000 rounds per gun

Bomb load: 5,511 lb (2,499 kg)

Speed: 219 mph (352 kmph) at 19,685 feet (5,999 m)

Ceiling: 27,890 feet (8,500 m)

Range: 1,740 miles (2,800 km)

Weight: 19,136 lb (8,679 kg) (empty); 27,392 lb (12,424 kg) (loaded)

Span: 74 feet 1 inch (22.58 m)

Length: 53 feet 9 inches (16.4 m)

Height: 13 feet 1 inch (3.98 m)

Crew: 5

The Heinkel He-111 was the standard Luftwaffe bomber at the time of the Battle of Britain. As a medium-range bomber, it was ideal for attacks on countries close to Germany, but it was disadvantaged by the distance it had to travel to reach targets in England. Among its features was a retractable firing point beneath the plane, in which a gunner sat.

Dornier D-17P1

Specification
Engines: Two BMW 132N 9-cylinder radials, 865 hp
each at take-off
Armament: Three 7.9-mm MG15 machine-guns
Bomb load: 2,205 lb (1,000 kg)
Speed: 246 mph (395 kmph) at 13,120 feet (3,998 m)
Ceiling: 20,340 feet (6,199 m)
Range: 1,367 miles (2,199 km)
Weight: 12,400 lb (5,624 kg) (empty);
        16,887 lb (7,659 kg) (loaded)
Span: 59 feet 1 inch (18.01 m)
Length: 52 feet 9 inches (16.07 m)
Height: 14 feet 11 inches (4.54 m)
Crew: 4

The Dornier D-17 first saw service during the
Spanish Civil War in 1936. It was vulnerable to
attacks from above and below. Known as the
'Flying Pencil' because of its narrow fuselage, it
had a shape similar to the British Hampden
bomber's. As a result, many Hampdens were fired
at by their own anti-aircraft gunners, who
mistook them for D-17s.

Junkers Ju-88A-1 medium/dive-bomber

Specification

Engines: Two Junkers Jumo 211B-1 12-cylinder inverted-V inlines, 1,200 hp each at take-off
Armament: Four 7.9-mm MG15 machine-guns
Bomb load: 4,960 lb (2,249 kg)
Speed: 280 mph (450 kmph) at 18,050 feet (5,501 m)
Ceiling: 26,250 feet (8,001 m)
Range: 1,055 (1,697 km) miles with fuel in the forward bomb bay
Weight: 16,000 lb (7,257 kg) (empty);
23,600 lb (10,704 kg) (loaded)
Span: 60 feet 3 inches (18.36 m)
Length: 47 feet 1 inch (14.35 m)
Height: 17 feet 5 inches (5.30 m)
Crew: 4

The Ju-88 was the most versatile aircraft in the Luftwaffe. It served as a level bomber, a dive-bomber and a night fighter. It was also used for reconnaissance flights. During the Battle of Britain it served as a medium bomber. However, it was no match for the Spitfires or the Hurricanes.

Chapter 7
The Blitz

The war in the air over Britain continued that way for the next three weeks. During that time we scrambled, we fought, we came back. We lost more pilots and planes. Scotty grew in confidence on each occasion he went up, even bagging five kills himself.

I had two letters from Ma during that time, saying she was worried about me and also that there was still no firm news of Edward, although the War Office had written saying that *after this length of time it is regretted that it must be considered that Lieutenant Edward Smith had been killed in action, the whereabouts of his body unknown.* Ma, however, still clung to the fact that, because Edward's body hadn't been found, it meant that he was still alive somewhere, maybe in a German hospital or prisoner of war camp.

'Your Pa says we have to accept the worst', she wrote. 'He says we have to admit to ourselves that Edward is dead; but I find it so hard. I really will not believe it until I see Edward's body for myself.'

Meanwhile, we fought on. The Luftwaffe continued their campaign to try and destroy our airfields. Many times they were successful, destroying our planes on the ground and our runways. But many times they also paid dearly for that success as we shot down their bombers and their fighters. However, as more and more of our planes and pilots never returned, I couldn't help wondering sometimes if we could keep taking losses at this rate. The Germans just kept on coming back in even larger numbers; it felt like we were fighting an uphill battle.

Then, on the night of 7 September, Scotty and I were sitting in the Mess with most of the squadron, having a drink, when Tug came in with a face like thunder.

'The Jerries are bombing London,' he said.

We all hurried out of the Mess and stood on the airfield, looking towards the south-west. Even from this distance we could see the black sky above London glowing a dull red and hear the distant *crump crump crump* as wave after wave of bombs fell on the capital.

We stood there, wishing we could go up against the bombers, but there was nothing we could do because we risked getting shot down by our own anti-aircraft guns.

The anti-aircraft guns sited around London were the first line of defence against night air attacks. When they were blazing away, sending tracers into the night sky, they couldn't distinguish between a German plane and a British one.

We hardly slept that night. Next morning, as Scotty and I waited to go up, Tug told us the terrible news about the previous night's attack.

'I heard about it from my cousin in the War Office,' he said. 'The Germans bombed the whole of the East End of London right up to five o'clock this morning. Four hundred and thirty civilians were killed, with over one thousand six hundred seriously injured.'

Later that morning, 8 September, as we flew over the East End of London, we saw the signs of the devastation caused during the night. It was sickening. I'd seen the results of bombs before, but mainly the damage to our own airfields. Below me whole streets had disappeared, buildings flattened into rubble. Parts of the East End were still burning, a thick pall of smoke rising. Ships were smashed and broken at their moorings in the docks. The dockyards themselves were on fire. Acrid smoke drifted up into the sky from the wreckage of the warehouses as the stored timber, paint and chemicals smouldered, every now and then bursting into flame.

The Germans didn't come that morning, but they returned in the afternoon. We harassed them as best we could, and they certainly went back with fewer planes than set out, but there was no mistaking that London suffered badly.

That night the Germans came back for a another night raid. Once more we could only stay at our base and look and watch helplessly as London was bombed and burned. I thought of Ma and Pa in their house and wondered how they were. Were they safe? Had our house in Regent's Park been touched?

The pattern went on like this for the next three days: the Luftwaffe's heavy bombers attacking London during the night, and then coming back during the day, usually in the afternoon, when we would swoop up and meet them, each time flying further to try and intercept them before they reached London.

The only good thing about it, from our point of view, was that the Germans' concentration on bombing London kept them away from our airfields and prevented further aircraft losses. We'd lost a lot of planes on the ground to German attacks on our airfields.

As the daylight bombing raids increased, we flew more and more sorties, with more and more of our planes in the air at any one time. Soon we seemed to be spending all our time in our cockpits. It was hardly worth getting out when you knew you would be clambering in again minutes later to buckle up and take off.

It was impossible to grab much sleep at

night because of the bombing raids on London. Being so near the capital, we were constantly on the alert in case we were bombed ourselves.

So it went on. Barely any sleep at night. None during the day. And flying sortie after sortie against the enemy. The strain and exhaustion began to take its toll on all of us. A leave rota was worked out to give us a chance to get away from the base for twenty-four hours and unwind. Some of the chaps went away for their day and simply slept. Others did the exact opposite: they went to the parts of London that weren't being bombed, like the West End, and did the round of restaurants and nightclubs, and came back even more tired than when they went!

When 11 September arrived it was 327's Green Section's time for leave. Tug Banks headed north to see his wife. Scotty and I grabbed a lift with a pilot from 58 Squadron, Freddy Fox. Freddy was heading for London to sample the nightclubs.

'If I'm going to die tomorrow, then at least I'll die with a smile on my face,' Freddy chuckled as he drove.

I sat beside him and wondered what I'd find when I got back to Regent's Park. Would there be any word of Edward? Maybe, by some miracle, he would be there, though this didn't seem the time when miracles happened much.

Scotty was going to visit some relatives in Barnet, just north of London, so we dropped him off at their house first, and then continued into the centre, down the A1. The nearer we got to it, the greater were the signs of bomb-damage.

Many streets had been closed off. In some cases the wardens were worried that the half-ruined houses would suddenly fall down and kill people. In other cases the road surface had simply vanished and been replaced by great craters many feet deep.

Freddy dropped me off a few streets away from home. It was as near as he could get.

'See you back at Hornchurch, old chum!' he grinned cheerily before driving off.

I picked my way over rubble and around craters. Some of the crushed buildings were still smouldering; obviously they had only been attacked in the previous night's air raid. I turned the corner and stopped, my heart frozen. There was just a pile of rubble where our house should have been.

Chapter 8
Bitter Words at Home

'John!' a woman's voice called.

I turned and saw one of our neighbours, Mrs Danvers, hurrying towards me. She was a tall thin lady of about fifty. When I had been a small boy she'd always appeared to be ancient, mainly because of the old-fashioned way she dressed: lace collars and long skirts. As I grew older, Mrs Danvers never seemed to age. She'd always been kind to me and Edward, always finding sweets for both of us. Nothing had ever seemed to disturb her, but now she looked deeply upset.

'I thought it was you.' she said. 'Terrible, isn't it? We were hit last night. Well, not us particularly, but the street.'

'Ma and Pa . . . ?' I asked, gesturing at the ruins of our house.

'They've gone to your Aunt Louise's,' said Mrs Danvers.

'Both of them?' I asked.

It was a stupid question but I was still in a sort of daze. Looking at the rubble, I found it hard to believe that they'd survived.

'Yes,' she said. 'Luckily they were in the Anderson shelter next door, at Mr Page's. They'd gone there because they thought he was frightened on his own and needed company.'

Some people had made their Anderson shelters quite comfortable. Mr Page was one of them. He'd got a couple of armchairs and a table inside it, with an oil lamp so he could read. I thanked Mrs Danvers for her news and then hurried off to my Aunt Louise's.

Aunt Louise was my mother's elder sister. She had a small flat in Gloucester Place, about a mile away from my parents' house. I could imagine that having to stay with Aunt Louise would only make Pa more irritable than ever. He was used to living in a large house and having his own things around him. To have to stay in three tiny rooms with someone else, even if it was his sister-in-law, would certainly put him in a bad temper.

Pa was out when I arrived at Aunt Louise's; just Ma and Aunt Louise were sitting having tea.

'John!' said Mum, her face lighting up as she saw me. She gave me a big hug, then she got all flustered as she looked round the tiny flat. 'You might have told us you were coming,' she reprimanded me. 'We could have made arrangements for you to stay somewhere tonight.'

'Sorry, Ma,' I said. 'It was all short notice.'

'Leave the boy alone, Amanda,' said Aunt Louise. 'Putting him up here is no problem. He can sleep in the hallway, if he doesn't mind draughts. I can put a rug and some blankets down for him.'

'Sleeping in the hallway will be perfect, Aunt Louise,' I said. 'It'll be a lot more comfortable than sleeping in the cockpit of a Spitfire, which is what I seem to have been doing most of lately.'

Aunt Louise poured me out a cup of tea and found me some sweet biscuits, which I wolfed down. Sweet biscuits were becoming a rarity in wartime Britain, as were many other things, such as chocolates. German attacks on the merchant-ship convoys had all but stopped the import of raw sugar.

We were sitting chatting – mainly Ma telling me about the house being bombed – when Pa arrived, back from his walk. He grunted and just nodded when he saw me. Aunt Louise went off to get another cup for him.

'The city is in a mess,' he muttered. 'Bombed buildings. Roads ruined.' He looked at me accusingly. 'I thought your lot were supposed to be protecting us?'

'We're doing what we can,' I countered. 'The Germans have got more planes than us. More pilots too. And although we can go up against them in the day-time, it's out of the question at night. I don't know why you don't all go out to the country,' I added. 'Uncle Stephen's got a big enough house down in Wiltshire. You could all go and stay with him while this is going on.'

'That's what I suggested,' said Ma. 'I told him my brother would be happy to have us, but your Pa absolutely refuses.'

'Of course I refuse!' he snapped. 'If the

king and queen won't let themselves be driven out of Buckingham Palace by this upstart Austrian corporal, then I'm damned if I'm going to run away.'

'It's not running away,' I said. 'It's just common sense.'

'We're not going, and that's that,' said Pa.

There was a heavy brooding silence for a few moments. Pa sat deep in thought, I stared out of the window, and Ma and Aunt Louise were afraid of saying anything that might upset my father.

Then Pa suddenly looked at me and snapped, 'Of course, if you fly boys had done your job properly at Dunkirk we wouldn't be in this mess.'

I stared at him, stunned. 'What do you mean?' I demanded.

'Boys, boys,' said Ma in soothing tones. 'This is not the time to argue.'

'I'm not arguing,' said Pa stiffly. 'I'm just stating facts. The RAF didn't give proper cover to our troops on the ground at Dunkirk. If they had, our troops would have been able to fight back and the Germans wouldn't be across the Channel right now, ready to invade.'

This was just too much. Despite Ma's appealing glance at me, I responded angrily. 'That's just not true!' I said. 'The RAF gave as much support as they could. They bombed German artillery positions and kept the Luftwaffe at bay. If it hadn't been for the RAF the losses at Dunkirk would have been even greater than they were!'

'Of course you'd say that, you're one of them!' my father growled. 'You fly boys have no idea of what real fighting is like. Bombs dropping around you. Trenches full of men drowning in mud. Hand-to-hand fighting. You lot just fly around the sky popping at each other from a safe distance.'

I could feel myself getting very angry thinking of Dob Masters and all the others who had died while serving their country and saving the lives of people like my father.

'Please, you two,' pleaded my mother, 'this isn't our house. Let's have no arguments.'

For my mother's sake I held myself back. Pa, too, decided he'd said enough and he just sat there, glaring into his tea cup. I knew that he was angry with himself, for the wound in his leg which kept him out of active service, but it didn't make me feel any better towards him.

The rest of the time passed in an awkward silence, with Ma and Aunt Louise making small talk, and Pa and I doing our best to avoid each other. That was difficult, though, in Aunt Louise's small flat. I felt that I couldn't stand the strain between myself and my father any more. I knew I'd have to go out somewhere, even if it was just for a walk. I didn't fancy spending the whole night cooped up with Pa. And then the air-raid sirens went off and let me know that I wouldn't have to. The Luftwaffe's bombers were on their way. London was under attack again.

Chapter 9
Underground

The four of us hurried to the nearest shelter, in the Underground station at Baker Street. The siren continued, a two-tone wail rising and falling, filling the air. Pa moved as fast as he could, but I could see that he was having difficulty because of his bad leg. I went to help him, but he brushed me away with an angry, 'Leave me alone! I'm not a complete invalid!'

Once again I bit my tongue and kept my silence. I turned my attention to Ma and Aunt Louise, but they were already walking fast along the street, but without appearing to rush. We were now part of a procession of people, all heading for Baker Street station. What struck me was how well-behaved most people were. As we got nearer I could see the steel-hatted figure of an air-raid warden, urging everyone on: 'No rushing, please! Keep it orderly!'

We reached Baker Street station and hurried down the stationary escalators to the platforms below. There an astonishing sight met my eyes. I hadn't realized just how well Londoners had adapted the Underground to meet the needs of bomb shelters. Some families had marked out their territory on a platform with tables and chairs. Even some beds had been brought down. There was a general atmosphere of good humour and helpfulness among the people.

We had barely reached the platform and found a place to sit, when the bombs began to fall. Even though we were so far underground, we could hear them explode, a mighty crash that made the walls shake and vibrate.

'Those are the big ones,' explained Aunt Louise to me, almost as if she were giving a lesson to a child. 'We don't hear the smaller ones.'

'Our warden says the incendiary bombs are the worst,' added Ma. 'They start fires, and when there's a wind they can spread from building to building within seconds. Whole streets burnt out within minutes. And there's no escape.'

I thought back to the time my plane had caught fire and I'd been able to bale out. No such possibility of escape for someone caught in a burning building.

'Then there are these terrible new things they're dropping –' Aunt Louise added.

'Land mines,' said my mother.

'Yes, those things,' said Aunt Louise. 'Honestly, John, they are absolutely huge. They drop them by parachute so that they don't go into the ground. That way, when they blow up, they do more damage. One of them came down in Marylebone Road but it didn't go off. I went to look at it. It must have been at least twelve –'

'Eight,' corrected my mother. 'They're eight feet long.'

'Well, they're certainly very big,' said Aunt Louise. 'As big as a small lorry.'

I could only sit there and marvel at these two elderly – to me, at least – ladies calmly discussing different sorts of bombs that were falling on them as if they were talking about new hats or new dinner recipes.

The walls reverberated as more and more bombs dropped. Heaven knows what sort of devastation was going on outside. I felt sorry for the men and women of the Civil Defence patrols and the fire brigades, out there in the middle of it, doing their best to put out the fires and to pull the dead and the wounded from the collapsed buildings.

Even down here I didn't feel safe. I expected the roof to come crashing down at any moment and all of us to be buried.

Suddenly, from further along the platform, I heard the sound of a mouth organ strike up a tune. I recognized it as 'Pennies From Heaven', which showed someone had a sense of humour. People started to sing the words, smiling at the thought that the only thing raining down on them at the moment were thousands of tons of German bombs. After 'Pennies From Heaven', someone started singing 'Roll Out the Barrel'. Other songs followed throughout the first few hours of that night underground, everyone singing to drown out the constant noise of the bombs and to keep their spirits up. The small children and babies who'd started to cry with fright as the first bombs fell gradually quietened down as the community singing continued.

Eventually, despite the thuds and explosions of the bombs, people began to sleep, curled up or lying flat out on the platform. Soon the singing died away and underground London slept, with the rhythmic crashing of the incessant bombing above them as a lullaby.

It was six o'clock the next morning before the All Clear sounded, a steady two-minute blast on a siren. We came out of the depths of Baker Street tube, bleary-eyed, and saw a city devastated. Looking at the heaps of rubble, the torn and burning timbers, the broken glass, I could only marvel that we'd survived the night at all.

Pa went with Aunt Louise back to her flat, while I walked with Ma to the ruins of our house in Ranelagh Place. We were going to sort through the wreckage and see if we could find any of the family photographs that she was missing. In particular I knew she was looking for the one of Edward that had been in a silver frame on the sideboard in the sitting-room.

As we walked, Ma tried to talk about Pa. She made excuses for him and the way he was with me: it was things like the pain in his leg, and worrying about Edward. I let her talk, although I knew that deep down he had never forgiven me for not following him and Edward into the Fusiliers. Pa was stubborn, but so was I. I was sure it was my stubbornness that had kept me alive in my aerial battles.

Ma and I reached the wreckage of our old house and we began to sift through it, pulling off rafters, moving bricks. Mr Page saw what we were up to and came out to help. So did Mrs Danvers. Before I knew it, the rest of our street was helping Ma and me comb the wreckage.

We found lots of things: a canteen of silver cutlery that had been a wedding present to Ma from Pa's parents, pieces of china, all broken. And then I found it: the photo of Edward in its silver frame, the glass miraculously not even broken. I also found a photograph of the pair of us, Edward and me when we were small boys. I gave them to Ma and watched her wipe a tear from her eye and give a little smile.

'Finding that photo of Edward is an omen, Amanda,' announced Mrs Danvers. 'It's a sign telling you he's still alive.'

'I know he is,' said Ma quietly, looking at the photo. 'Edward's out there somewhere. He'll come back to me, I know it.'

I gave Ma a big hug. 'And wherever he is, he knows you're thinking of him,' I said.

To be honest, I didn't know whether Edward was alive or dead. All I knew was that finding the photograph had made her happy, and for the moment that was all that mattered.

Mr Page came over and joined us. 'If we find anything else, I'll keep it safe in the Anderson shelter for you until you come back,' he told Ma.

We thanked him, and Mrs Danvers, and all the others. And then I walked Ma back to Aunt Louise's, her carrying the two photographs, me carrying the canteen of cutlery.

After that, there wasn't much left for me to do in London, so I headed back to Hornchurch and back to battle.

Chapter 10

Back into Action

Next morning I was in my deck-chair at the base, waiting to be scrambled into the air. Tug Banks came and sat himself down beside me and asked, 'Everything all right, Bonzo?'

'Fine, skipper.'

'Only you looked a bit lost in thought. Everything go OK on leave?'

'Fine,' I said. 'Our house was bombed.'

'Bad show. Folks bearing up?'

I nodded. 'They were sitting in next-door's shelter playing cards when it happened. They're fine.'

'Good,' he said. He looked reflectively up at the sky, in the direction we knew the German planes would come from. 'My wife's feeling a bit under the weather with all this,' he said. 'She worries about me. I keep telling her I'll be fine; I'm like a cat with nine lives, but you know what wives can be like.'

I nodded. I didn't, but it seemed the thing to do.

Scotty arrived beside us, also casting long glances into the sky, searching for incoming enemy planes. 'London took another terrible hammering last night,' he said.

'Our only hope is that the Jerries will overstretch themselves,' said Tug thoughtfully. 'Bombing day and night, it must be wearing their pilots out.'

'Maybe they'll give themselves a rest today?' said Scotty hopefully.

It was a thing we all said many times, and it always seemed to work like a bad luck charm. As so many times before, the sound of the siren told us that today was not going to be a quiet day. We were already out of our chairs and heading for our planes as the voice of Control came over the loud-speaker: 'All pilots in the air. Repeat. All pilots in the air. Attack fleet coming.'

I reflected on his 'all pilots in the air' instead of just scrambling one or two sections. It must be a huge attack force on its way. And it was.

We ran into them just south-east of London at 14,000 feet. A huge formation of planes. The sky was black with them.

As I saw the lines of bombers with their fighter escorts, pictures of London flashed through my mind, things that I had seen of the damage done by the bombs: the dead bodies, the wreckage, the flattened buildings. I vowed that these German bombers would have to fight hard to get past me again.

The sky was now full of planes. As well as our two squadrons from Hornchurch, 327 and 58, we had been joined by other Fighter Command 11 Group squadrons from Rochford, Biggin Hill and Kenley. Hawker Hurricanes and Spitfires from those bases flew with us as we united against this formidable enemy formation, the Heinkel, Dornier and Stuka bombers accompanied by their Me-109 guards. All told there must have been two hundred German planes heading towards us, the biggest air attack I'd yet encountered. The sheer size of it almost took my breath away.

Luckily, there was no time for any of us to dwell on it.

'Plenty for everyone, chaps!' came the voice of our squadron leader over my headphones. 'Let's go! Free attack! Just hit the blighters!'

The danger with so many planes in the air was of hitting another plane. There are no brakes in a plane: if you found yourself heading on a collision course, you had to change direction, hoping this didn't put you in someone else's path.

We dodged the Me-109s as best we could and poured burst after burst of bullets into the German bombers. Just hitting one was no guarantee that it would go down. They were well built, I'll say that much for them.

Soon the blue sky was thickly patterned with black-and-white criss-crosses of smoke, adding to the chaos. There was no time to pause to keep a tally of who had shot down what; it was just fly, fire, hit, run, fly back and fire and hit again.

I flew over one of the Heinkels, strafing it with a burst of machine-gun fire, and then turned for a return attack. Out of the corner of my eye I saw a Me-109 coming straight for me from behind. I dived in time and its bullets flew over my head, chipping bits off the hood of my canopy.

I climbed back up to get a height advantage. As I did so I saw Tug in Green One zoom past me. He turned and gave me a wave and a thumbs-up.

Suddenly, directly in front and just above him, I saw a Me-109 that had been hit crashing down out of the sky, flame and black smoke pouring from its engine. It was on a direct course to collide with Tug. Frantically I pointed and Tug looked up. He saw the falling Messerschmitt and put his Spitfire into an abrupt dive, banking heavily at the same time. But it was too late; the burning plane hit one of Tug's wings, tearing it off.

Immediately he went into a spin, spiralling down out of the sky. I tore after him, ready to cover him if he baled out. I saw him trying to slide back the hood of his cockpit, but it had stuck, just like mine had weeks earlier.

Suddenly a Me-109 came out of nowhere from behind me. The first I knew of it was tracer bullets hurtling past me and smashing into Tug's plane. As I watched, Tug threw up his arms, and then his plane blew up, exploding in mid-air, throwing out flames and gases and bits of fuselage.

I turned to go after the Messerschmitt, but one of the Hurricanes was already on to it. The Hurricane pilot put a burst into its rear, tearing off the rudder, and the German fighter plunged into a spin, fire and smoke belching out from its tail.

A second or so later the Messerschmitt pilot baled out, his parachute blossoming out wide as he began to float down towards the ground. For a moment I was tempted to let him have it right there, to let my bullets tear into him as he drifted in the sky, but I stopped myself. It was one of those unwritten rules of aerial combat: you only shot at a man when he was in his plane; you didn't hit him when he was dangling helpless from a parachute in the sky. Not even if he'd just killed your friend.

By this time the German fighter planes must have begun to run low on fuel because they all began to turn, heading out towards the sea. The large bombers, with no escorts to protect them, also turned. What was left of the German formation, about 150 planes, began their journey home.

'Back to base, chaps!' came the voice of our squadron leader in my headphones.

I headed back to Hornchurch. As I flew I counted the planes that were left of the twenty-four Spitfires of 327 and 58 Squadrons that had set out just half an hour before. There were sixteen of us. Eight down. Some of those would have parachuted to safety, or brought their damaged plane down to land somewhere in the countryside below. But not Tug Banks. Tug Banks was dead.

Chapter 11
Invasion Alert

That evening I was sitting in the Mess, drinking a cup of tea. I'd left my meal half-finished; I just didn't feel like eating. Scotty, too, just pushed his food around the plate. We both felt badly about Tug buying it, but somehow neither of us felt like putting it into words, apart from the occasional 'Poor old Tug.'

I was just about to go out for a walk to try to get my feelings sorted out, when Squadron Leader Jerry Payne came into the Mess. He walked over to me and clapped me on the shoulder. He was still dressed in his flying kit.

'Acker wants a word with you,' he said. 'He's waiting for you in his office.'

'What does he want?' I asked.

'I'll let the wingco tell you himself,' he said. 'Don't keep him waiting, there's a good fellow. Chop chop.'

I left my tea and hurried across the base to the wing commander's office.

Wing Commander 'Acker' Atkinson was busy writing at his desk as I tapped at his half-open door. He was a grizzled old character, a veteran of the First World War. Tough, but fair.

He motioned me to come in.

'You sent for me, sir?' I said, standing to attention before him.

'At ease, Smith,' said Acker. 'You're not on the carpet for anything. In fact, the exact opposite. I've just been discussing the situation at Green Section with Jerry Payne. I'm sorry about Banks; he was a damned fine pilot and a great section leader.'

'The best there was, sir,' I said. 'I was proud to have flown with him. He saved my bacon on a number of occasions when I was first up, cutting out Jerry plenty of times when they could have taken me out.'

'I know,' nodded Atkinson soberly. 'The thing is, we need a new leader for Green Section, and Payne and I think you're the man for the job. As of this moment you're promoted to Flight Lieutenant.'

I suppose I should have seen it coming. With fewer and fewer experienced pilots able to go up, it had to be one of the existing members of the squadron. It still felt a bit sour to me, though, promotion by dead man's shoes, as we called it, especially when the dead man had been a good friend.

'Thank you, sir,' I said. 'I shall do my best to live up to your confidence in me.'

'You'd better,' smiled Acker. 'We need your experience up there.'

'Will I be getting a third pilot for Green Section?' I asked. 'Or will it be just me and McBurn?'

'Fighter Command have promised me a third pilot for you by first thing tomorrow morning. I don't know his name yet, but we'll find out by Assembly Call. There's a briefing of all section leaders first thing tomorrow morning, zero five hundred hours. Early start tomorrow. You'd better get some sleep.'

He stood up behind his desk and shook my hand.

'Dismiss, Flight Lieutenant Smith.'

'Thank you, sir,' I said.

By the time I got back to the Mess, Jerry Payne had already told everyone the news about my promotion, and there was much slapping me on the back and murmurs of 'Well done, young 'un. You deserved it,' and similar sentiments from the older and more experienced pilots. Proud though I was of my promotion, it was still tinged with sadness that I'd earned it at the death of a friend.

I accepted a congratulatory drink from young Scotty. Then I hung about in the Mess just long enough not to offend all the other chaps who wanted to buy me a drink in celebration. Once things had quietened down a bit I sloped off quietly, with a murmured 'Goodnight' to Scotty. His nod showed me that he understood that I wanted to be on my own.

Outside the Mess I looked up at the night sky. At the stars. At our battleground. And sadly I reflected that tomorrow there'd be one less great pilot flying up there. Another friend gone.

Five o'clock the next morning, 15 September, found the section leaders from 327 and 58 Squadrons sitting attentively in the Briefing Room. For the very first time, I was one of them. Acker Atkinson finished chalking a rough map on the blackboard. It showed the coasts of northern France and southern England.

'Right, chaps,' he said. 'All of you are familiar with this. You've flown over it often enough. The difference today is that – if our Intelligence reports are right, and it looks as if they are – you're all in for the biggest battle of your lives, and instructions have come down from the top brass to tell you why. They think it's only fair, and I agree with them.'

He picked up his pointer and tapped along the chalked outline of the French coast.

'The German invasion fleet has now been ready here for some days. According to Intelligence reports there are three thousand boats there, all ready to cross, with thirty German divisions. If they don't land here by late September then the tides will be against them and the invasion will have to be postponed. Possibly even cancelled altogether. But the Germans can't invade until they're sure we're out of the way.

'Apparently Goering promised Hitler that the RAF would be completely smashed by the start of September and the way would then be clear for the invasion. Two weeks later, and we're still here, to Hitler's immense distress and annoyance.

'Our Intelligence people believe the Germans will now throw everything they've got at us, starting today. I don't believe I am exaggerating when I say that you are all that stands between victory or defeat in this war. We have to defeat the Luftwaffe in the air today, and over the next few days. If we lose then the Nazis will have the final piece in their jigsaw map that is Europe.'

He looked at his watch.

'It is now zero five thirty. The enemy are expected to launch their attack within the next two hours. Prepare your men, prepare your planes, and good luck.'

Chapter 12
The Battle for Britain

I headed towards the Mess to grab a bite of breakfast before the balloon went up. Not too much food, of course: it didn't do you good to have your stomach overfilled when you were being thrown this way and that way, sometimes even upside-down, during the course of an air battle. As I walked in I saw Scotty talking to a young, fresh-faced, red-haired kid still dressed in his blues.

'Bonzo, this is Stephen Byways,' Scotty introduced us. 'Byways, this is our section leader, Flight Lieutenant John Smith.'

'Pilot Officer Byways reporting, sir.' He saluted as he stood stiffly to attention. 'I've been assigned to Green Section of 327 Squadron.'

'Relax,' I said.

It made me feel a little uncomfortable. Here was this young lad standing to attention, saluting me and calling me 'sir'. It made me feel as if I was about fifty years old instead of nineteen. Out of the corner of my eye I saw Scotty grin at my obvious discomfort.

'How old are you?' I asked.

'Eighteen and a half.' He added: 'I've been fully trained.'

'Good,' I said. 'Have you got your flying kit?'

'Not yet, skipper.'

'He's only just arrived,' Scotty explained. 'He came down by lorry last night with the new intake.'

'OK,' I said. 'Scotty, take Byways to the stores and get him kitted out. Then show him his plane and get him ready for action. Afterwards he can have some breakfast.' I gave the young lad a smile, so he didn't think I was being too hard on him. 'I'm not being mean, but if the scramble suddenly goes, it's quicker to run straight to your plane from the breakfast table than to have to start getting your flying kit on first.'

'Roger, skipper,' Byways nodded. He looked deadly serious as he said it.

'Come on, let's get you fixed up,' said Scotty.

I watched them go and thought how much older we must all look to Byways. Battle does that to men, it puts years on their faces.

After breakfast, I sat outside the Mess in my deck-chair. When Scotty returned with our latest recruit, Byways had on the regulation pilot's flying gear.

'Excellent,' I said. 'Get some chow and then sit out here while Scotty and I tell you how to save your life while fighting Jerry up in the blue yonder.'

On his return, Scotty and I gave the boy what advice we could about what he would need to know when the German attack came.

I let him have the same pep talk that I'd given Scotty when he'd joined our squadron: about not letting yourself be caught out and blinded by the sun, about watching your back, about doing your level best to keep calm. However, as I sat there I could only think, 'Nothing we can say will help this boy when it happens. We can't fly his plane for him. If he panics when the fighting starts and turns the wrong way, or dives or climbs too sharply and blacks out, there's nothing I can do to help him.' When you're a fighter pilot, you're on your own. Finally all I could do was pat him on the shoulder in what I hoped was a comforting gesture and tell him, 'Do your best to stay alive up there and just hit the opposition as hard and as often as you can.'

Then we waited. There was a definite sense that today was going to be something special. It was as if all the previous weeks of battles in the air had been leading up to this, the final struggle. I imagined that at every airfield across England the same scene was being played out. Pilots sitting around, all kitted up, their planes at the ready. Checking their watches. Making jokes about the enemy being late, but everyone feeling that today there was just that little bit more tension, just that little bit extra tight knot of fear in the stomach.

0800 came and went. No sign of the enemy. The loudspeakers remained silent. Maybe they weren't coming today? Maybe

Hitler had decided to cancel the invasion altogether? Wild thoughts like these passed through our heads, even though we knew they were out of the question. Too much was at stake. The battle had been fought too long and too hard, with too many losses, for the final chapter to be avoided.

0830 and still no sign. No radar warnings. Nothing.

The minutes ticked by. For heaven's sake, I thought, hurry up. This waiting is worse than the fighting! Looking at the tense faces of the other pilots, I knew they felt the same as I did, even the older hands. Byways, who was going up into battle for the first time, could barely sit still. Every now and then he got up and walked about, and then sat down again.

0845. Still no sign. Surely they had to come soon.

0850. By now the airfield was so heavy with silence you could almost have heard a pin drop. And still there was nothing from the loudspeakers. No call to scramble. No word of the enemy.

At 0900 hours we finally got it: 'Scramble all planes. Enemy approaching.' As we ran to our planes we almost cheered with relief. At last!

At 0915 we ran into them coming over the east coast at 12,000 feet. Intelligence had been right about the size of this attack: it was the biggest force I'd seen. The sight was just absolutely staggering. There were about four hundred German fighters protecting some two hundred bombers. The sky was thick with German planes.

'Green Section, stay close to me in V-formation,' I told Scotty and Byways over the radio.

'Read that, skipper,' they both responded.

We were in a pack now, spread out from north of the Thames right down to the south coast. There must have been at least two hundred Spitfires and Hurricanes in the air. Our aircraft were from every station, from both Groups 11 and 12. A formidable force, even so we all knew we were heavily outnumbered.

I went into the attack straight away, leading Scotty and Byways behind me as I headed for the nearest bomber, a Dornier.

'I'll take the Me-109, you two hit the

bomber,' I said. 'Go for the pilot at the front.'

I flew head on, on a collision course, for the Me-109 that was riding shotgun for the Dornier on the near side, firing all guns. The German pilot must have decided that I was obviously mad enough to commit suicide, because he went into a climb.

I turned as sharply as I could and followed him. As he began to turn to look for me, I caught him in my sights and let fire with tracer that tore his starboard wing apart.

Out of the corner of my eye I saw Scotty and Byways still attacking the glazed front of the Dornier, weaving two criss-crossing trails of white smoke in the air as they dodged the machine-gun fire from the bomber's forward gun. There was no doubt about Byways's flying ability or his courage. Young as he was, he flew at the bomber and hit it again and again, until the glass was so cracked I knew it had to go. I also knew from experience that the crew behind the glass were either dead or badly wounded. Sure enough, a few seconds later, the Dornier began to go down. One less bomber.

The sky was filled with similar battles

going on. The Germans had sent over enough fighter planes this time to allow some of them to be released to engage our Spitfires and Hurricanes in individual combat, and all around individual dogfights were going on. Every few moments there was an explosion near by, with black smoke pouring from another wrecked aircraft.

Planes filled the sky. Smoke obscured our vision. Time and time again I saw two planes collide and burst into flames. It was just mayhem and madness, and all we could do was dodge and weave and attack and hope we wouldn't bump into someone else.

After about twenty minutes of this, the sweat was pouring down my face and my helmet felt sticky, even though it was cold at this altitude. I could understand why some pilots preferred not to wear goggles in case they misted up.

I did my best to keep an eye out for Scotty and Byways, but it was almost impossible in the clutter of planes whirling around the smoke-filled sky. Finally some of the German planes began to turn back as they ran low on fuel. Jerry Payne's voice came over the radio ordering our squadron back to Hornchurch for refuelling.

'Back to base, 327!' he chirped. 'They'll be back. Plenty more for later. Time to fuel up.'

We turned home, leaving 58 Squadron in the sky with many of the other fighters who were still attacking and harassing the German planes that had stayed. Once we were refuelled we'd go up and carry on the defence in the air, and 58 could come down.

While the ground crew refuelled my plane, I hurried to meet our newest pilot as his plane taxied in. He tumbled out of his cockpit and lifted his goggles.

'Well done, Byways!' I congratulated him. 'You showed you've got guts and skill up there just now. Hang on to them and you'll be OK!'

'Thanks, skipper!' he said with a nervous smile. 'It's pretty crowded up there, isn't it?'

'It's busier than usual,' I said. 'You joined on a bad day.'

'No,' grinned Byways, 'this is a good day. What's the point of being a fighter if no one turns up to fight you?'

'True,' I said. 'But don't get too confident.

We're not fighting amateurs up there, you know. These Germans are experienced and battle-hardened. Get too cocky and make one mistake, and you'll be dead.'

'Point taken, skip,' nodded Byways. 'Thanks.'

Refuelled, we went up into the air again.

And that was how it went on all that day. More German fighters, more German bombers, and us in the skies doing our best to stop them reaching London, or stop them reaching our airbases. For so long it just seemed like a never-ending nightmare. As fast as we shot them down, more German planes appeared.

By the time we went up for our fourth defensive foray, with still no sign of the German attack lessening, we were beginning to get exhausted, both physically and mentally. The sky was now a mixture of cloud and burning smoke. Even inside the cockpit, with your oxygen mask on, you could taste it, acrid and choking.

As we went up we saw a wave of twenty Dorniers and Heinkels coming in over the east coast with their Me-109 escorts at

10,000 feet. Twenty Me-109s and twenty bombers. Forty planes in all.

Behind them was another wave of at least thirty Stukas, followed by another twenty Messerschmitts. Behind them, at least four hundred planes. The German attack seemed to be endless.

The thought of the heavy bombers devastating London again filled me with a cold anger. I checked that Scotty and Byways were close to me and asked our Squadron Leader for permission to take Green Section to attack the bombers.

'All yours, Green Section,' came Jerry Payne's voice over my radio. 'We'll take the Stukas.'

'Green Section, with me,' I said.

Scotty and Byways followed me as we broke away from the rest of our squadron. Outnumbered forty to three, there was no way we could go for a head-on attack, so I flew in an arc which took us behind the first wave of bombers and fighters. While Red and Blue Sections joined the other squadrons in attacking the next formation, Green Section went in hard on the tails of the first German wave.

I set my sights on the Dornier at the rear of the German formation. Even as I let fly with a burst of tracer, the bomber's Me-109 escort turned to intercept me. Before he could get a fix on me, Byways came at him, flying so close that for a moment I thought he was going to crash into the German fighter. Byways's bullets smashed into the front of the Me-109, destroying its engine. Meanwhile Scotty and I had both hit the Dornier with bursts into its tail-plane. The bomber lurched abruptly, then its tailplane disintegrated and the huge plane tipped and dropped. Two down.

From then on it was fight and fly, bullets pouring from our guns into the Germans as they flew dangerously past our planes. Time stopped there in the sky. There was just gunfire. Explosions. Smoke. And machines whirling and swooping everywhere.

Four of the Me-109s riding shotgun had decided that we needed to be dealt with, and they turned to come straight for us.

'Up, Green Two and Three!' I ordered.

Scotty and Byways soared up, while I headed swiftly down. I turned, then came up from underneath and let one of the

Me-109s have a burst of fire in its belly. I banked and came back and hit another side on, raking along its fuselage. Meanwhile Scotty and Byways had dived down on the other two Me-109s, hitting them from above, their bullets ripping along them from rudder to propeller.

'Right, let's get the bombers!' I said. 'Break formation. Don't let them get a fix on you.'

We flew wide of each other to come in on the bombers from different directions, guns firing. The German machine-gunners opened up and a burst from one of the Heinkels tore jagged holes in my Perspex canopy, missing my head by inches. Our sudden attack had thrown them, though, and we hit two of the bombers, their engines bursting into flames and sending the huge machines spiralling down to earth.

By now the Germans' fuel was running low and the survivors of this wave turned their planes and headed for home. We chased them out over the sea, firing at them all the time. Then we turned and flew back to join the rest of our squadron, ready to face the next attack.

And still the Germans came, wave after wave of them.

By six o'clock that evening we hadn't had time to stop for a bite to eat, just a quick cup of tea from a mobile canteen when we'd scrambled down from the cockpits of our planes during refuelling.

As the light faded from the sky and the last wave of daylight raiders returned home across the Channel, we flew back to our bases to count our losses, leaving south-east England to the protection of the anti-aircraft guns and the barrage balloons.

I felt bone-weary as I clambered down from my Spitfire for the last time. We had kept the enemy at bay for another day. I checked that Scotty and Byways had landed safely, and then headed towards the Operations hut to report Green Section's tally of kills.

Afterwards, as I walked toward the Mess finally to grab something to eat, I found myself being hailed by Crusty Pearson. What is it now? I thought. Crusty Pearson always meant trouble of some sort.

'There's a visitor for you, sir,' Crusty announced crisply. 'In the wingco's outer office. You'd better get over there.'

I was frowning as I reached the wing commander's hut. Who on earth could be visiting me? And why? I found out as I opened the door and went in. There, alone, was my father.

For once he wasn't standing in that military stance he always had, that stiff back, chest-out parade-ground pose. He looked suddenly old, his shoulders sagging slightly. The thought hit me in an instant: he'd come to tell me that something terrible had happened to Ma. She'd been killed in the bombing.

Chapter 13
Alive!

'Hello, Pa,' I said, steeling myself for the bad news. To help him say it better, I asked: 'Is it Ma?'

He shook his head.

'No, John. Your Ma's fine. And so's Edward.'

Edward? I stared at him, stunned. Then I could feel a grin spread all over my face. Edward was alive!

'That's wonderful news!' I blurted out. But I was puzzled. If it was all good news, what had brought him all the way out to Hornchurch? And why did he look so unhappy? The answer came with his next few words. He limped over and stood facing me, pushing his shoulders back. It was as if he had made a difficult decision.

'John,' he said, 'I've come to say sorry. Your Ma said I could write it in a letter, but I wanted to come and tell you face to face.'

'Sorry?' I repeated, bewildered. This wasn't like my father at all.

'For the things I said and the way I acted,' he said. 'I was unfair towards you. And towards the RAF. You didn't deserve it. And the RAF didn't deserve it. I was quite wrong.'

'Well,' I began, feeling stuck for words, not knowing what to say. This was all coming completely out of the blue.

Pa handed me an envelope.

'We'll talk in a minute,' he said. 'First, read this. It's from Edward. I came to give you this so you'd know yourself he's all right.' He hesitated, then he added, 'I'll wait for you outside.' He gave a self-conscious smile. 'I always have preferred showdowns in the open air.'

I took the envelope from Pa and watched him limp out of the wingco's office. Then I took out the letter and read what Edward had written.

Dear Ma and Pa, Edward began. *Well, I guess I've caused you a lot of worry. I'm writing this from up here somewhere on the coast of Scotland. I've just landed from a trawler. The first thing I heard when I got in touch with my unit was that I was officially dead, so I thought I'd get this off to you straight away, to let you know that I'm not. I tried phoning you but the Post Office say your phone is out of order.* I smiled at that, wondering what Edward would say when he found out that it wasn't just the phone, it was the whole house that was out of order. The letter went on to describe how he'd been wounded and had hidden. Then he wrote:

All the time, though, I was getting word about what was happening back in Blighty, and about the terrible hammering the Jerry bombers have been giving you. Everyone in Norway and up here in Scotland is talking about what a magnificent job our RAF boys are doing keeping Hitler's flying circus at bay. Heroes, every one of them. And that includes John. If you see him, give him my love and tell him I admire enormously what he and his fellow boys in blue are doing. I'm sure you've been telling him this all along, Pa, but be careful about giving John too

*much praise. We don't want him to get a big
head just because he's a hero!*

I looked up from Edward's letter and out
through the window to where my father was
standing on the grass, with his back to me,
gazing at the planes and the waiting air-
crews. I wondered how he must have felt
when he read that phrase of Edward's
about not praising me too much in the light
of the insults he'd thrown at me. I returned
to Edward's letter.

*I hear that Winnie – all right, Pa, Winston
Churchill; I know you don't approve of me
being disrespectful about our Prime Minis-
ter, even if it's done with affection – I hear
that Mr Churchill gave John and the other
RAF fighter pilots the biggest praise when
he said of them: 'Never in the field of human
conflict has so much been owed by so many
to so few.' Just about sums it up, eh?*

*Anyway, enough of all this. I look forward
to seeing you both soon. All my love, your
loving son, Edward.*

I folded up the letter, put it back in the
envelope and went out to where Pa was
waiting for me. I handed Edward's letter
back to him.

'I'm so glad he's safe,' I said. 'I'll try and get some leave and get home when he arrives back.'

'Your mother would like that,' said Pa. Then he added, 'I would like that.' He shook his head, still looking guilty, and continued: 'I was blind about what a good job you were doing, John. All of you flying boys. I don't know whether it was because I was still upset you didn't go into the Fusiliers, or worry over Edward being missing, or a combination of them all. All I know is, I was wrong. It took a letter from one of my sons to make me realize how proud I was of both of you. Can you forgive me?'

In that moment I wanted to go to Pa and give him a big hug, the way I used to when Edward and I were very small, but I knew that would be going too far for him. He was an old soldier, a colonel, and I was his son, the airman. And we were on public view.

'There's nothing to forgive, Pa,' I said. 'But I can't tell you what it means to hear you say it, and to know that you came all the way out here.' I smiled in an effort to try and lighten the moment. 'To an RAF base.'

Pa caught the mood and gave me a smile

back. He held out his hand, and I took it firmly in mine.

'Here's to the Army and the RAF,' he said.

'Here's to the family, Pa,' I said. 'Together.' My voice was almost lost in the roar of a Spitfire flying overhead.

The Battle of Britain and After

The Battle of Britain itself culminated on 15 September 1940. That day – now remembered as Battle of Britain Day – saw the last major attack by the Luftwaffe against the RAF, a last-ditch attempt to gain air supremacy and clear the way for the sea invasion. On 16 September bad weather prevented the Luftwaffe from launching another large-scale attack, and on 17 September high winds again thwarted an attack. It was also now doubtful if the Luftwaffe could launch a further decisive attack anyway. Following the sustained period of air battles with the RAF over England, the German pilots were exhausted, spares for their planes were in short supply, bomber units were depleted, and morale was at a low ebb. They had been assured by German Intelligence that the RAF had hardly any fighter planes left to oppose them. Yet on 15 September three hundred RAF fighters went into action against them over southern England. Between 7 and 30 September the Luftwaffe lost 380 aircraft against RAF losses of 178.

On 17 September, as a direct result of the failure of the Luftwaffe to destroy the RAF by 15 September, most historians believe Adolf Hitler postponed Operation Sea-Lion. Two days later he gave the order for the German invasion fleet to be dispersed. Britain had avoided the imminent threat of surface attack.

The Blitz on London by the German Luftwaffe continued until early November 1940, a total of fifty-seven days of continual bombing, starting on 7 September. There was just one break, on 2 November, when the weather was too bad for the German aircraft to take off. London was not the only British city to be a victim of the German tactic of aerial Blitzkrieg. On 14 November Coventry was devastated by bombers, then

Southampton, Birmingham, Cardiff, Swansea, Liverpool, Plymouth, Portsmouth, Bristol, Glasgow, Belfast and many other towns. During these raids, which continued until May 1941, 40,000 British civilians were killed, another 46,000 injured and more than a million homes were damaged. Despite this massive bombardment, Britain remained undaunted and undefeated.

What Happened Next?
The resistance shown by the RAF during the Battle of Britain had a crucial impact on the outcome of the Second World War:

• It stopped the Germans from being able to launch their sea invasion of Britain, which would have ended the war in 1940 and given Hitler complete domination of Europe.

• It raised the morale of the British people, and of others throughout the world, who now saw that Hitler's military might could be defeated.

• It led to Hitler turning his attention away from invading Britain to invading Russia. This led to Russia being brought into the war on the side of the Allies, a major factor in the final defeat of Nazi Germany in 1945.

The Battle of Britain

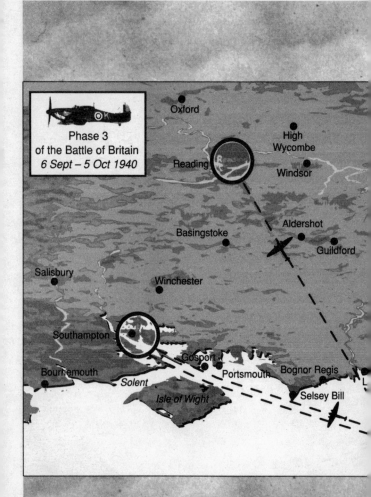

Phase 3
of the Battle of Britain
6 Sept – 5 Oct 1940

Oxford

High
Wycombe

Reading

Windsor

Aldershot

Basingstoke

Guildford

Salisbury

Winchester

Southampton

Bournemouth

Gosport

Solent

Portsmouth

Bognor Regis

L

Selsey Bill

Isle of Wight

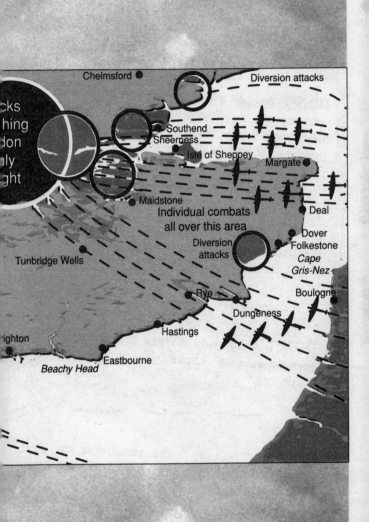

Pilots Beware

These are some of the official 'hints and tips' given to pilots, including cartoons, as supplied by the RAF during the Battle of Britain.

DON'T go into a combat without goggles over your eyes. Splintered glass is not good for them, and some Pilots are now paying extra Insurance Premiums for their cars.

DON'T go off without your goggles, gloves and flying boots. They are a great help in case of fire in the cock-pit.

DON'T wind your oxygen tube around your neck. It may choke you if you have to "bale out."

DON'T "beat up" the aerodrome on your return, however pleased you are with yourself. It is bad manners, and some of those aerodrome defence chaps might take it the wrong way.

DON'T FORGET THESE

Civilians at War

NOT TRANSFERABLE

City of Westminster

Admit person named below for

PICCADILLY STATION

Issued subject to the London Regional War...
...29.12.40, and 73...
...copies of which are exhibited at the stations.

Name... FLORENCE SADIE JESSOP Age 32

Full Postal Address... 10 STURGEST BORO SEI

Nature of Employment... HOUSEKEEPER

Signature of above person... F. JESSOP

Parker Morris.
Town Clerk and A.R.P. Controller.

Date 3. 12. 1940

Signature of Issuing Officer... [SEE BACK]

USE YOUR STATION QUIETLY AND REGULARLY. HELP TO KEEP IT TIDY AND CLEAN

During the Blitz many Londoners took shelter in the Underground.

Civil Defence

COUNTY OF WEST SUFFOLK

AIR RAID PRECAUTIONS.

This is to certify that the Bearer

Douglas L. Christian

is an Air Raid Warden for the
COUNTY OF WEST SUFFOLK
(Rural Districts).

W. D. Robertson ...Captain,
Chief Constable.

Signature of Holder D. L. Christian

Air Raid Warden's identity card.

What was it actually
like to fight as a
commando in the jungles
of Burma? Watch out for
the next gripping
Warpath book, *Behind
Enemy Lines* . . .

Night-time in the jungle. I lay hidden in the
long grass. About fifty yards in front of me
was a river, crossed by a rickety wooden
bridge – a vital link in the Japanese supply
line. My task was simple: to blow the bridge
up. I was Lieutenant John Smith of 142
Commando. I was on my own because a
large force would be spotted more easily
than just one man. In the bag slung around
my neck was my equipment: timer pencils,
wire and plastic explosives, all wrapped in
waterproof oilskin. I was light on weapons,
with just a Colt automatic pistol and my
fighting knife.

Ahead of me trees, bushes and long
rushes lined the muddy riverbank.

I decided to attack the bridge from
upriver. The current would take me down-

stream to the supports holding up the middle of the bridge.

Keeping flat, I edged forward, digging in my elbows and knees to zigzag like a snake slowly through the grass.

There were guards patrolling the bridge, the moonlight glinting on the barrels of their rifles. Ten yards to go before I made the cover of the riverside trees. Eight yards. Five. Four. Then I was among the trees. Crouching low, I moved towards the water.

Suddenly I glimpsed a movement out of the corner of my eye. Before I could turn and defend myself, a boot behind my knee knocked my legs from under me. The next second I was sprawled face down on the ground, one arm pulled savagely and painfully up between my shoulder blades, the sharp blade of a knife pressed against my throat. A voice rattled out '*Sayonara!*'